THE DUKE'S
RELUCTANT BRIDE

Newly Duke of Hathersage, Colonel Elliott Bromley is obliged to marry one of the old duke's brood in order to release his inheritance. Vivacious and impertinent Lady Rosamond, the second daughter, most definitely wishes to remain a spinster — just five years more and her own inheritance will grant her the independence she needs to establish herself as a novelist. But one of the sisters must wed the new heir to keep the estate in the family — and Elliott has chosen Rosamond . . .

FENELLA J. MILLER

THE DUKE'S RELUCTANT BRIDE

Complete and Unabridged

LINFORD
Leicester

First published in Great Britain in 2013

First Linford Edition
published 2015

A catalogue record for this book is available
from the British Library.

ISBN 978–1–4448–2300–4

Published by
F. A. Thorpe (Publishing)
Anstey, Leicestershire

Set by Words & Graphics Ltd.
Anstey, Leicestershire
Printed and bound in Great Britain by
T. J. International Ltd., Padstow, Cornwall

This book is printed on acid-free paper

1

London 1814

'Have you run mad, Bromley? You cannot agree to these terms — they are outrageous.' Lord Peter Davenport thumped the table to emphasise his point.

'I have no choice, Davenport. The terms of the will are quite clear — unless I marry one of the old duke's daughters, all I inherit is the title. Already the various estates, and his unfortunate family, are unable to meet their bills because the money is tied up.'

'I can't understand it. If you were his heir, why in God's name did he not get in touch with you and give you the opportunity to learn how the estates are run?'

'He had a perfectly good heir until three years ago when the unfortunate marquis broke his neck in a riding accident. His legal team were unable to contact me as I was busy fighting Bonaparte. Then the duke contracted a wasting disease and kicked the bucket last year.'

'Why have none of these girls had a season and been presented at court? Did you not say they are between sixteen and twenty-two years of age? One would have thought they would sail off the marriage shelves at Almacks, being both aristocratic and heiresses. Surely they can't all be bracket-faced?'

'No doubt the two oldest girls would now be spoken for if first their brother, and then their father hadn't died and plunged them into mourning. Something I didn't tell you, which makes it even more imperative I follow the dictates of this extraordinary will — the three sisters won't have a dowry until I have married the fourth.' Elliott, once plain Elliott Edward Bromley, but now the eighth Duke of Hathersage, Lord

Bromley, stared gloomily into his glass of claret.

'Good God! Are you to dance attendance on the other three whilst they preen and primp at soirees and balls? You'll never do it — Bromley, I see no option but to volunteer my services until you've got shot of the other three.'

Elliott laughed. 'I don't suppose you would like to take the Dowager Duchess under your wing as well? From what I've gathered she is a formidable lady with the shape of a plum pudding and the stare of a basilisk.'

'You know nothing about running a vast estate, or indeed about being a top-of-the-trees aristocrat — let alone doing the pretty with a parcel of young ladies. How in tarnation are you going to pull this off successfully?'

'I was a colonel in the rifles — have brought the scum of the earth into line and made them the best damn soldiers in Wellington's army. I intend to approach my new command in exactly

3

the same way.' He yawned and his jaw cracked loudly. 'I'm away to my bed. If you wish to accompany me you'd best do the same. I've decided to ride to Hathersage; from my reckoning it's no more than twenty miles from London.'

His friend and fellow comrade in arms pushed himself upright, upsetting both glasses of claret. The dark stain spreading across the damask cloth sent a shiver down his spine; he'd seen too much blood spilt over the past five years and didn't wish to be reminded of the unpleasantness.

'Good grief, Bromley, you can't turn up on horseback — you're a duke now and should arrive in style. You know how important first impressions are — '

'Enough of that nonsense, Davenport. I don't give a damn what they think of me. We none of us have any choice in the situation. I've spoken to the lawyers and have all the necessary paperwork. All that remains is to decide which one of the chits will make me the best wife.'

'Presumably your carriage will take our luggage and valets?'

'Of course, but they'll make slower time, so be prepared to manage without a manservant when we arrive.'

As they strolled from the private parlour of the coaching inn, Elliott slapped his friend on the back. 'I'm relying on you to help me make my selection. I'm a rough soldier and know nothing about young ladies of quality. I don't care over much about the girl being beautiful — but I could not spend the rest of my life with a woman with no more sense than a pea goose and no interests apart from replacing her wardrobe and attending parties.'

'All four are titled and will have been educated to run an establishment such as yours. The two youngest won't do for you, as they are scarcely out of the school room, and you're already past your prime.'

'I'm nine-and-twenty, not in my dotage. However, your reasoning is sound.' His laugh echoed around the empty vestibule. 'Reducing the field to two possible brides makes my life so much easier. I'll make a devilishly poor husband for either of them — they must be dreading my arrival as much as I am.'

'You are over two yards tall in your stockings and have all your teeth, a handsome face, and a full head of dark hair. In addition you're now as rich as Croesus, and the Duke of Hathersage. All four of the young ladies in question will be desperate to be your bride, even the youngest of them. You will be fighting them off with a stick.'

'Good night. Be ready to depart at dawn.' He grinned at his friend's horrified expression. 'Being a civilian has turned you into a milksop, Davenport. Four hours' sleep should be enough for both of us. Be grateful it's June and the weather's perfect for our journey.'

* * *

Hathersage Hall

Rosamond hurled the branch into the lake and her dog, a hairy, overgrown black dog of indeterminate ancestry, dived in after it with scant regard for his owner. 'Calli, you stupid animal, I'm quite drenched.' She laughed and shook out her sodden skirt, hoping it would dry before she was obliged to return to the hall. Mama would have a conniption fit if she saw her now — appearances were everything to her parent.

Calli — short for Caliban — snatched up the branch and swam strongly back to shore. This time she was ready and ran backwards, allowing him to shake himself without receiving more water on her gown. The dog bounded towards her and dropped his offering at her feet, then barked, demanding she throw it again.

'Well, once more. I'm so wet it really can't get any worse.' This time she didn't approach the edge and thus avoided the deluge which followed as he jumped in for a second time. This would probably be the very last time she could please herself what she wore and where she went; the only advantage of being the daughter her mother disliked was that she was mostly ignored. She and her sisters would be under the control of the new head of the family, who was expected to arrive that very afternoon.

Amelia, known as Millie, was older than her by two years, and beside herself with excitement at the prospect of becoming a duchess. Millie was certainly the most beautiful of her sisters, with corn-coloured ringlets, sky-blue eyes, a perfect figure and a sweet nature. She would make a perfect wife for this recently elevated soldier.

Flora and Elizabeth were equally determined they would catch his eye. Her younger sisters might only be sixteen and seventeen years of age, but they were well aware they would never have such an opportunity to find themselves the perfect husband. They were both almost as pretty as Millie.

Rosamond, on the other hand, was profoundly grateful she was neither blonde nor blue-eyed, but had hair the colour of a rodent, muddy green eyes, and stood a head taller than all of them. She was the antithesis of the current fashion for diminutive golden young ladies, and she had no intention of marrying anyone if she could avoid it. Her lack of countenance and unfashionable colouring must put her at the bottom of the list when it came for the new duke to select his duchess.

Papa had arranged that her trust fund would become hers when she was five-and-twenty. This meant she merely had to avoid matrimony for a further five years and she would be free to live the life she craved. She intended to be a writer of fiction; she was an avid reader and had already penned two novels of a romantic nature which she was sure would be enthusiastically received when she was able to publish them.

This, of course, couldn't take place until she was in her own establishment. If anyone were to discover her secret she would be a social outcast, for well-bred young ladies did not, under any circumstances, indulge in such rackety pastimes as writing novels.

Since dearest Papa had gone to meet his maker more than a year ago, life at Hathersage had been decidedly difficult, for without the new duke the lawyers had been unable to release the funds to pay the bills. Millie was the only one to have had any new gowns, as Mama believed her golden girl must always keep abreast of the latest fashions.

Rosamond had been delighted that their lack of funds meant that even though the period of mourning was long gone, they were still not entertaining. Mama refused to make morning calls, or to set up a house party, whilst they were in such straits.

The man who had inherited everything was a cousin, but the connection was so distant as to be almost invisible. However, he was the second son of a cousin of a great-uncle, or some such thing, and thus his title was clear. Mama had learnt a little about this unknown gentleman and none of it had filled her with enthusiasm. He had been a professional soldier all his adult life and knew nothing about running a big estate or managing money.

Rosamond laughed out loud and her dog barked at her. Her mother and sisters might think him beneath their touch, someone who would need to be told in no uncertain terms how to behave, but she couldn't wait to meet him. He would bring a welcome breath of common sense to their rarefied existence.

She was ready to be his friend and offer him any assistance he might need to negotiate the tricky waters of Hathersage, but that was all she was prepared to do. If he showed the slightest interest in her she intended to behave appallingly, dress outrageously and give him such a disgust of her that he looked elsewhere for his bride.

After spending another hour raking about the woods, she decided to visit the stables and check that her beloved stallion was improving. Foolishly he had jumped out of his paddock to find her and, in the resulting chaos as the grooms attempted to catch him, he had cut his hind leg. He was now confined to his box until fully recovered, which suited neither of them.

She approached the stables from the tradesman's entrance, her hair in disarray, her oldest gown mud spattered and still damp, her face in no better state, without a care in the world. All those who worked at Hathersage were used to her hoydenish ways and treated her with as much civility and respect as any other member of the family.

The head groom touched his cap and bowed. 'Sultan is much improved, my lady. I reckon you'll be able to ride this afternoon.'

'Thank you, Albert. I'll take him out

after luncheon — unless his grace has arrived by then.' The horse had heard her voice; his massive brown head was craning over the stable door and he was stamping and whinnying impatiently.

'I'm coming, silly boy. Don't make such a noise.' She embraced him and he slobbered happily on her shoulder. 'Step back, Sultan. I wish to inspect your injury.' All she had to do was press lightly on his shoulder and he moved obediently. He was a massive horse, but had impeccable manners — a veritable gentle giant.

She was busy inspecting his flank when she was interrupted by the clatter of hooves and a sudden flurry of activity in the yard outside the loose box. A deep, authoritative male voice froze her to the wall. Surely not?

Fate could not be so unkind as to send the duke to the stables when she was dressed like a ragamuffin. She edged her way to the half-door and carefully peeped around to see two tall gentlemen dressed alike in smart riding coats and buff breeches conversing with Albert.

She knew at once who the duke was, for Albert was tugging his forelock and bowing repeatedly to the dark-haired man. His shoulders were broad, his hair cut in the modern style, and he was hatless. Another point in his favour — for she disliked wearing a bonnet above all things. Indeed, did not Mama constantly complain about this very thing? His companion was of slighter build but his hair was equally dark. She wondered who he was. No doubt another military gentleman, for they both had the upright bearing of soldiers.

Then, to her consternation, the duke began an inspection of the dozen horses that were in residence. There were as many animals turned out to enjoy the summer sunshine as there were in the stable yard. Papa had always treated his horses well, making sure they were not overworked, and that the head groom rotated the stock to ensure that all had time to graze in the lush home paddocks.

Whilst the duke was at the far side of the yard she might have time to slip out and make her escape without being seen, but he gave the carriage horses no more than a cursory glance and then headed to her side of the yard. Sultan shoved his head out and whickered a greeting. Immediately he headed towards her horse.

'Albert, this is a magnificent animal — to whom does he belong?'

'This is Sultan, your grace. He belongs to Lady Rosamond. He was a name day gift from the late duke for her tenth anniversary. He was bred and broken here — he might look a handful for a young lady, your grace, but he's as sweet as a lamb with her ladyship.'

She held her breath, expecting to hear the duke's condemnation; for him to say such a massive stallion was no fit ride for a lady. Instead he said something quite unexpected.

'I cannot wait to meet Lady Rosamond

— she must be a bruising rider.' He patted Sultan and strolled off, leaving her strangely shaken by the almost encounter. A few moments later Albert appeared at the loose box entrance.

'All clear, Lady Rosamond. If you go round the back you should get in safely enough without being seen.'

'I was terrified he would come in and find me — thank you for not revealing my presence here. My ride will have to wait until after dinner. I'll send word when I'm coming.' She sighed. 'I suppose I'd better ride side-saddle. It wouldn't do to upset the duke so soon in our acquaintance.'

The indoor staff were well used to her sudden appearances in their domain and barely paused from their tasks as she skidded past the kitchen and the servants' hall, and up the back stairs that led eventually to her apartment on the first floor. This being a relatively modern house, the bedchambers were all upstairs and the various reception rooms, dining rooms and drawing rooms were on the ground floor. The servants' accommodation was in a separate wing on the east side of the massive edifice.

On the west side was the guest wing, where there were a dozen or more apartments which were only occupied once or twice a year when the Christmas and summer house parties took place. There had been neither of these enjoyable events since her brother had died three years ago.

Jane, Rosamond's personal maid, was beside herself. 'My lady, his grace has arrived and you're needed downstairs immediately. I have your gown ready, and there's hot water. We must be quick; the message came a while ago.'

'I think we have half an hour at least. The duke came on horseback and will wish to attend to his appearance before he presents himself.' She giggled as she threw her soiled garments in a heap on the floor. 'Although as his luggage has yet to arrive. The most he can achieve is polished boots and sponged jacket.'

'I've chosen the green check muslin

with the emerald sash, my lady. It brings out the green in your eyes.'

'It's a great shame it cannot do something for my lack of womanly curves, Jane. I fear the gentleman might find it impossible to distinguish my front from my back.'

'My lady, you should not say such things. You are tall and slender, but none the worse for that. And your hair might not be golden curls, but it is wondrously lustrous and such a pretty colour.'

'Mouse brown is not especially attractive — but I agree it does have a lovely shine and a satisfactory wave as well.'

When her hair was freshly brushed and arranged, she quickly stepped into her clean gown. She viewed herself in the full-length glass and nodded. 'Thank you, Jane. As usual, you have worked miracles and I look almost pretty. I shall, as always, look like a cuckoo in the nest, but I'm satisfied I can look no better.'

She ran along the spacious passageway to the gallery, pausing there to look over the balustrade, hoping to catch a glimpse of the new owner of all this magnificence. Her mother, resplendent in lavender silk, was flanked by her three sisters: Millie, looking exquisite in pale blue dimity, on her right, and Flora and Elizabeth in matching pastel muslins on her left.

She had never understood why the good Lord had thought fit to make her look like an alien amongst her siblings — Papa had said she was the image of his grandmother, whilst her sisters favoured Mama's side of the family.

The staircase on the left of the vast vestibule that led from the guest wing remained empty. With luck she would be in her position next to Millie before her tardiness was noticed. A slight sound behind her made her turn.

'Good afternoon. I believe I have the pleasure of making the acquaintance of Lady Rosamond, do I not?'

2

Rosamond meant to curtsy and respond politely that she was also pleased to meet him. However, she spoke what was on her mind. 'I should have remembered you would be this side of the house. I do apologise, your grace, but might I ask you a small favour?'

He nodded gravely. 'I am at your service, my lady.'

'Thank you. Do you mind remaining up here for a few moments longer so that I can join my sisters and my mother in the hall? Mama will never forgive me if we arrived together.' She grinned. 'And neither will my sisters.' He raised an eyebrow and she giggled. 'For me to have met you first would be disastrous — tantamount to Cinderella meeting Prince Charming.' She clapped a hand to her mouth in horror. 'Good grief! No sooner do I open my mouth than both feet go firmly in it. I did not intend to infer — '

He laughed, but managed to smother it with his hand. 'I understand perfectly, Lady Rosamond. Now, for how long must I lurk on the gallery before descending to greet the rest of my new family?'

'Two minutes. Just give me time to grovel for my tardiness and place myself tidily beside Millie.' She didn't wait for him to respond but gathered her skirt and ran down the stairs. She skidded to a halt and curtsied to her parent.

'You are late, Rosamond, and your cheeks are flushed. Why can you not be an obedient daughter like your sisters and not give me constant palpitations?'

Rosamond mumbled her apology and hastily stepped in beside Millie, who squeezed her hand sympathetically but didn't dare commiserate out loud. Millie took several deep breaths, unclenched her fists and checked her gown was hanging smoothly. Her sister tensed beside her. The duke, their legal guardian and head of the household, must have appeared on the gallery.

Rosamond raised her head and straightened her spine and glanced towards the stairs. She had half expected him to pause dramatically and allow his new dependents to study his magnificence before descending. Instead, he stopped halfway down and called out to them: 'This banister looks perfect for sliding down — I really cannot resist it.'

To her mother's horror, her sisters' astonishment and her amusement, he swung a leg across the polished surface and launched himself backwards. He hurtled around the curve. She held her breath, expecting him to crash on the tiles, but miraculously he managed to vault from the banister and land neatly on two feet.

'Bravo, sir. That was impressive.' Rosamond clapped, and after a second's hesitation so did her sisters. Only her mother remained in stony silence.

He strolled across the vast expanse of black and white tiles as if nothing extraordinary had taken place. He bowed to Mama. 'Duchess, I apologise if my unorthodox arrival has upset you, but I'm not a man to stand on ceremony. I intend to continue to live my life as I please and not be dictated to by unnecessary convention.'

Rosamond feared her mother might explode. Eventually she managed to respond. 'I sincerely hope, sir, that you do not wish to disregard the hundreds of years of tradition that have served this family well. Hathersage has always been a serious place and such frivolity is out of place.'

His expression changed. He was no longer light-hearted but a formidable, grim-faced soldier. 'Madam, I am sure that I do not have to remind you that you live here at my whim. How I conduct myself in my own home is entirely my business.'

'And I'm sure that I do not have to remind you, sir, that without marriage to one of my daughters you own nothing. A title is all very well, but without the wherewithal to maintain it you will make a sorry figure indeed.' Mama turned on a heel and stalked off, although being rather short and dumpy the effect was somewhat spoiled. Her sisters glanced nervously at the duke and then scurried after her.

Rosamond remained where she was. She must try and placate him before this confrontation became an all-out war. 'Your grace, I must explain . . . '

'No, my dear, you must not. This whole debacle was entirely my fault. When I saw you all standing to attention as if waiting for inspection, I thought to lighten the mood and totally misjudged the situation.' He smiled and raised his hand as if he were going to touch her face, then let it drop. 'What should I do to put matters right?'

'Nothing at all. Just come down to dinner and behave as if nothing untoward has happened. Be charming, be civil, but on no account apologise.'

'I shall do as you suggest, Lady Rosamond. Should I introduce myself to your sisters or wait until then?'

'Mama will brood in her sanctuary — the yellow drawing room. I shall round up my sisters and take them for a stroll in the rose garden. Why don't you and your friend do the same?'

He nodded. 'Which reminds me — Davenport should be down by now.' He lowered his voice. 'Is that fearsome gentleman approaching us the butler?'

'It's Gibson. He's a stickler for rules and etiquette. The housekeeper is Turner; no doubt she will present herself shortly. We didn't expect you until this evening and the entire staff were to be assembled on the steps to greet you.'

'Then I'm thankful I arrived unannounced. Such flummery is not for me.' She was moving away when he called her back. 'Lady Rosamond, I met your stallion earlier. The animal is far too large for you, but I am prepared to reserve judgement on his suitability until I've seen you riding him. When do you intend to take him out?'

'In one hour, after I have introduced my sisters to you.' She nodded briefly and escaped before she said something she would regret. How dare he suggest he might take Sultan away from her? He had been given to her by Papa as a colt and they had broken him in together. The horse was her last link to her beloved father and she would never relinquish him.

Her sisters were twittering together in the music room. 'Come along, girls. I have it on good authority the duke is going to inspect the rose garden. I have introduced myself and shall do the same for you.'

'He's not at all what I expected,' Millie said. 'Mama has taken him in dislike, but I think I might come to like him very well.'

'I'm delighted to hear you say so, as you are going to be the one to sacrifice yourself on the altar of matrimony.'

Flora pouted. 'I like him too. I shall set my cap at him. He's a trifle larger than I would like and very noisy, but being fabulously rich and a duke is ample compensation for his shortcomings.'

'And what about you, Elizabeth? Do you wish to be considered?' Rosamond waited expectantly for her youngest sister to give her opinion.

'I don't wish to marry him after all. Either Millie or Flora can have him, and then I'll have a magnificent season and find my own husband.'

As usual her sisters didn't consider Rosamond to be in the running, and she was tempted to pretend an interest, but thought matters were complicated enough already. 'Excellent. Let's hope he's not as pig-headed as Mama and doesn't withdraw from the race because he's in high dudgeon.'

The French windows opened onto the terrace and she led the girls outside and chivvied them towards the rose garden. The duke and his friend were nowhere in sight.

★　★　★

Elliott adjusted his neck cloth and smiled ruefully. Not an auspicious beginning — he'd managed to offend the entire family plus most of the senior staff. That was a record even for him. His friend greeted him from the right side of the gallery.

'What have I missed? Where is everyone? I expected to be introduced to your new family and maybe select a leftover bride for myself.' Davenport sauntered down the stairs and joined him in the vestibule.

'Where the hell have you been? I'm sure I wouldn't have made such a cake of myself if you'd been here.' He regaled his companion with his exploits and they were both laughing when they emerged into the sunlight and headed for the rose garden.

'Which of the girls are in contention? Did you have time to give them all a thorough inspection?'

'Actually I've made my decision. I won't tell you who it is; wait until you've met them all and can hazard a guess.' He'd known the moment he had set eyes on her which one would be his bride. She was the antithesis of everything a young lady aspired to be — but petite, demure, golden-haired girls didn't appeal to him. Although this would be a marriage of necessity, at least married to Rosamond he would not be bored. She was outspoken, intelligent and headstrong, and he was going to enjoy bringing her to heel.

When he announced his decision her appalling mother and simpering sisters would be outraged. The girl was used to being overlooked, and being chosen over her sisters would be a novel experience. That she would be over-joyed to be his duchess went without saying; he couldn't wait to inform her and see her fine eyes light up with joy.

★　★　★

Flora saw them first. 'The gentlemen are coming, Millie. Shall we pretend we haven't seen them, or wait expectantly

29

as we were before?'

'I don't know, Flora. What do you think, Rosamond?'

'Behave naturally. I don't believe that either of them stand on ceremony and won't appreciate you treating them like royalty.' Her sisters looked at her as if she had taken leave of her senses. 'Until two weeks ago the duke thought himself a commoner, a colonel on half pay with a modest income from his spoils of war. I doubt he's had the opportunity to change into a high-in-the-instep aristocrat in the interim, do you?'

She turned to face the gentlemen, and her sisters gathered round her like golden chicks around a brown mother hen. She pinned on a smile, determined not to show that she had taken a dislike to the duke for his high-handed attitude. His companion was even more handsome than the duke. His eyes were blue and were a delightful contrast to his dark hair.

'Lady Rosamond, what a pleasant surprise. Would you do me the honour of introducing your beautiful sisters?'

'This is Amelia, this Flora, and this Elizabeth. Girls, allow me to introduce his grace, the Duke of Hathersage. I am unable to introduce his companion as I haven't yet been introduced to him myself.' This veiled criticism of the duke's manners didn't go unnoticed.

His strange tawny eyes glinted. He was not amused. He half-bowed to her sisters. 'I am overwhelmed to make your acquaintance. The talk in town of your beauty has not exaggerated the reality.' He nodded to Rosamond. 'Allow me to introduce Lord Peter Davenport. He was my aide-de-camp throughout the Peninsular Campaign and is my closest friend.'

There was further bowing and curtsying and then the introductions were complete. Both the duke and Davenport seemed bowled over by the beauty of her sisters, and Rosamond thought it safe to leave the gentlemen in their hands. She slipped away whilst they were engaged in animated conversation and hurried back to the house to change into her riding habit and escape to the stables. She couldn't wait until after dinner to ride.

Jane sent a chambermaid with a message that Sultan be saddled and waiting for her. Whilst her maid was pinning on her military-style cap at a jaunty angle, she thought it pertinent to ask what the gossip below stairs was. 'How have the staff viewed the arrival of the duke? He can hardly be more different from my father or grandfather.'

'They are divided as to their opinion, my lady. The senior staff are not impressed, but the younger members think he will make an excellent job of it.'

'I'm sure he will; however, I wonder how many of our neighbours he will upset before he's accepted? If he careers around the countryside in the same giddy way he slid down the banisters, they will likely think him fit for Bedlam.' She nodded at her reflection. The moss green of her ensemble made the best of her meagre looks. She tilted her head to one side. Yes — today her eyes were greener and her hair more attractive than usual.

'There, my lady, you look a picture. Do you wish me to select your evening gown, or do you have a preference?'

She hesitated. She had intended to wear her least flattering dress, one that Mama had chosen in a hideous buttercup yellow which made her skin look sallow. 'Perhaps the eau-de-nil. I don't believe I've worn that yet.' That this confection was in the first stare of fashion, had a plunging neckline and exquisite beading that flowed around the skirt and encircled the hem, was no consideration at all.

She collected her gloves and bone-handled whip and was ready. As always she took the servants' stairs, as they led directly to the back door, and she was less likely to be waylaid by a message from her mother demanding her attendance in her drawing room.

Sultan whickered a greeting as she appeared through the archway. He was tacked-up and eager to go, as it had been several days since he'd been exercised. 'Albert, in case anyone wishes to know, I'll ride around the park and back through the woods. I should be gone no longer than an hour; he can be turned out on my return if his cut has remained closed. I don't require a groom to accompany me, as I'm remaining within the park.'

'As you wish, my lady. This old fellow is that eager to go you'll need to give him a good gallop to settle him down.' Albert had known her since she was in leading strings; he had been closely involved with the stallion's schooling and understood her horse almost as well as she did.

'I intend to. He can stretch his legs along the back fields. The going is good and there are several excellent jumps to be had over the ditches.' Calli frolicked around her legs, expecting to be included in the treat. 'No, boy, stay here.' The dog retreated and flopped down in front of Sultan's loose box.

She preferred to mount using the block and not be tossed into the saddle by a groom. She gathered the reins, placed her left boot in the single stirrup iron and swung smoothly into the saddle. Although her horse wouldn't budge until she gave him the office, a groom stood at his head just in case, whilst she settled her right leg around the pommel and adjusted her skirt. Like many ladies she wore breeches beneath her riding skirt, which meant there was no danger of exposing any part of her anatomy if she took a tumble.

'Thank you, Billy. You may release him.' She clicked her tongue and touched the stallion with her heel and he moved away smoothly. His long stride covered the ground and within minutes she was on the broad ride that completely encircled the park.

Hathersage was set in over one hundred acres and the majority of this was woodland and pasture, but the park in which she intended to ride was a mere twenty acres. 'Now, Sultan, you may canter, but you shan't gallop until we reach the meadows.' She slackened the reins a fraction and sat back in the saddle. The horse lengthened his stride into an easy, collected canter. He made no effort to increase his pace; he was completely in tune with her and would only gallop when told he may do so.

At the end of the ride she pulled up and swung around to check his injury hadn't opened after the activity. Satisfied everything was as it should be, she guided him towards the meadows, where she used the handle of her whip to open the gate.

Now she could give him his head. She checked the pins in her hat were secure and patted his shiny neck. His muscles bunched and when she tapped his shoulder, he surged forward. She crouched over his withers, loving the wild gallop, eagerly anticipating the three wide ditches she would have to jump.

The stallion stretched his neck. His ears were pricked and his huge hooves knocked divots into the air with every massive stride. They both knew where the jumps were; there was no need to tell him to prepare. Sultan steadied, shortened his stride and flew into the air, clearing the first ditch by yards.

He continued unchecked and she laughed out loud, revelling in the freedom and excitement. She urged him faster and he responded. They cleared a second ditch and galloped flat out towards the third.

To a stranger it might have seemed her huge horse was bolting and she unable to control him. Sultan would slow immediately if she touched the reins, but for the moment they were both enjoying the mad race.

Rosamond was readying herself for the final ditch when from nowhere another rider thundered up beside her. She just had time to glance sideways and saw the duke reaching out towards her as if he intended to snatch her from the saddle. Sultan ignored the intruder and, increasing his pace, they sailed over the final obstacle.

She gently pulled on the reins and sat back. Instantly Sultan responded, and by the time her unwanted companion rode alongside, her horse was in a collected canter. Only an imbecile could possibly have believed that at any time she'd lost control of her mount.

He reached out and grabbed her reins. He heaved on them as if her horse had a mouth of iron and Sultan, not unnaturally, took immediate offence. The stallion's head swivelled and before she could prevent it he sunk his teeth into the duke's leg. His language turned the air blue. Whilst he was trying to dislodge the stallion, Rosamond took the opportunity to show her displeasure by hooking her foot around his leg.

'Let go, Sultan.' The horse released his victim and, as he did so, she managed to remove the duke's boot from his stirrup. She then reached across and gave him a hefty push and was delighted to watch him topple from his horse. He was floundering on the grass but was still able to swear at her in a most ungentlemanly way.

If he carried out his threat to beat her she would be in for an unpleasant time.

She cantered away, determined to reach the safety of her bedchamber before he caught up with her. She shouldn't have tipped him from his saddle, but had acted on impulse. Papa hadn't agreed with physical punishment — and she prayed the man who had the legal right to beat her wouldn't carry out his threat.

3

Elliott watched the girl canter away as if she hadn't a care in the world. His fury turned to amusement and he was laughing out loud when his friend reined in beside him and dropped to the ground. 'God's teeth! Are you hurt, Bromley? It's not like you to take a fall.'

'Give me your hand. Lady Rosamond's beast took a lump out of my leg and it hurts like the very devil. I didn't fall; she pushed me from the saddle.' If he had stated he was the Antichrist, Davenport couldn't have been more surprised. 'For the second time today I have made a jackass of myself. I must take control of matters here whilst I still can.' His head was filled with an image of a slender girl with magnificent eyes and the misguided belief she could do as she pleased.

'I don't believe it! The girl's half your weight — I doubt if I could tip you out even if I wished to.' He grabbed Elliott's arm and heaved him upright. 'Did the stallion draw blood? I don't see any on your breeches.'

He gave his thigh a cursory glance but could see no more than the damp imprint of teeth. 'I'll live — in fact it's my pride that's hurt, more than my body.' He grinned as he reclaimed his horse and prepared to mount. 'I have a score to settle with that young lady and I'm tempted to put her across my knee. Don't look so scandalised, Davenport. I shan't do so.' He rammed his feet into the stirrup irons before continuing. 'I've a far better punishment in mind.' His friend didn't enquire what this was and changed the subject.

'I'm still at a loss to know which of the delectable young ladies you have chosen; on balance I think it must be the eldest, Lady Amelia.'

'You couldn't be further from the

mark. Lady Rosamond will be my wife. The others might be more beautiful but they haven't the character, wit or intelligence of their sister and would bore me into my grave within a year.'

When he clattered into the stable yard a while later he wasn't at all surprised to discover his quarry had flown. No matter — he would speak to her after dinner, but first he must make his peace with her mother and inform the redoubtable dowager of his choice. A large, friendly dog came over to greet him and he wasn't surprised to discover this also belonged to Lady Rosamond. It seemed she possessed a pair of unsuitable animal companions.

He spoke briefly to the head groom and, satisfied his orders would be carried out to the letter, he strode along the wisteria-draped path that led to the side door. He paused to stare up at the massive building. There must be more than a hundred rooms, of which only a handful were used on a regular basis. A vigilant footman threw open the door and bowed him in. He should inspect the staff; they would be expecting it. Whenever he had taken command of a new regiment the first thing he did was talk to the men under his command.

Instead of returning to his apartment he stopped in the centre of the hall and snapped his fingers. The sound echoed and Gibson, the austere butler, glided to his side. 'I wish to speak to the staff — have them assemble here in twenty minutes. Make sure the outdoor staff are included in the summons.'

As expected, his luggage had arrived and his man, Jenkins, who had been with him throughout his military career, had everything ready for him. He wasn't just his valet, but a comrade in arms and the most loyal companion a fellow could have. 'Your bath is waiting, your grace, and I told Gibson you wish to dine at five o'clock — none of these country hours for you.'

'It will have to be a quick dip, Jenkins. I'm speaking to the troops in twenty minutes. I might as well dress for dinner; by the time I've made a speech to the staff and made my peace with the dowager duchess, it will be almost five o'clock.'

He stripped in seconds, tossing his garments into the waiting arms of his valet, and was about to step into his bath when Jenkins spoke. 'Bugger me! You've got a nasty bruise, your grace. I'll fetch the arnica.'

'Lady Rosamond's horse took a lump out of me — entirely my fault. It's a bit sore, but nothing to worry about.' In fact his thigh was an interesting shade of purple and the indentations of the animal's massive teeth were clearly visible. He submerged himself briefly in the lemon-scented water and used the washcloth to remove any lingering soil from his journey.

Years of bivouacking on campaign meant he was able to complete his ablutions and get dressed in the required time. Jenkins took care of his clothes but he was quite capable of dressing himself and tying his own cravat. He favoured the simplest style; no elaborate 'waterfalls' for him. He didn't bother to check his appearance in the mirror, as he cared little for such vanity. High collars, striped waistcoats and such nonsense were for a macaroni, not an ex-soldier like himself.

This time he arrived in the hall in a more orthodox fashion. He remained three steps up so he could be seen clearly by all who were gathered there. There must be more than fifty indoor servants and the same of outdoor. The housekeeper had made those that had come in from the stable yard, garden and elsewhere remove their boots, and they were standing with grubby feet looking either embarrassed or disgruntled.

He scanned the crowd, letting his glance rest on each for a second, making them all feel they were included in his welcome. He thanked them for their industry and loyalty and gave them his word that they would be

45

secure in their employment as long as they continued as before. When he announced that all his staff would in future have a free half-day every week and a whole day once a month, a ripple of excitement ran around the gathering.

'I must not hold you back from your busy day any longer. Return to your duties and continue to give the excellent service to me as you have to my predecessor.'

Before Gibson could ask for a rousing three cheers, Elliot jumped from his position on the stairs and marched directly at the front line of maidservants. The crowd parted like the Red Sea and he was safely into the grand drawing room and closing the doors securely behind him with no hindrance.

Davenport was ahead of him. He, too, was smartly accoutred, and like him favoured the new fashion of evening trousers and slippers, rather than knee breeches and stockings.

'Any sign of the family? I have precisely half an hour to find my future mother-in-law and inform her of my decision. Then I must make a formal proposal to Lady Rosamond. I suppose champagne will be in order once the engagement is official.'

'According to the butler, the young ladies and their mama are expected momentarily to arrive. Shall I make myself scarce?'

'Absolutely not — I'm less likely to get a bear-garden jaw if you're at my side.' He positioned himself in the centre of the room so he would be immediately visible when the doors were opened. He wanted it clearly understood he was the master of this establishment and that his word was law. If he allowed himself to be browbeaten, the pattern would be set and he might find it more difficult to keep this household under his command.

'Brace yourself — enemy action imminent,' Davenport said as he positioned himself two strides to his right.

The double doors were pulled back and the dowager duchess sailed in, resplendent in maroon silk and matching turban with several bobbing egret feathers. The golden daughters fluttered behind her. Lady Amelia was gowned in a simple pink-coloured silk with a sparkling overskirt; she was without doubt the most beautiful young woman he'd ever set eyes on. The younger girls were dressed in floaty white muslin, one with a yellow sash and the other with a blue. Of his intended bride there was no sign.

*　*　*

Rosamond erupted into her private parlour, sending a large ginger tom straight up the curtains. 'Rufus, what are you doing up here? Bad cat — you're not supposed to come upstairs.'

Jane hurried in and made vague shooing gestures at the irate feline

48

hissing and spitting from his vantage point on the curtain pole. 'Oh dear, however are we going to get him down? He must have sneaked in when your hot water was being taken into the bathing room.'

'He must remain where he is for the moment, as I'm certainly not going to attempt to remove him. Perhaps he could be tempted down with a morsel of food?' She frowned at the unwanted visitor. 'I do hope this doesn't mean we have mice in my apartment. Have you seen any evidence of them, Jane?'

'No, my lady, not at all. One of the maids said that his grace doesn't wish to eat dinner until five o'clock in future. The kitchen is in turmoil at the very idea of such a late meal. At least you have ample time in which to get ready so you can take a leisurely bath this time.'

When Papa had installed baths in a separate room for each apartment it had been a nine-day wonder in the neighbourhood. He had explained to her how the waste water flowed through the pipes and out into a special soak away, and thus saved the chambermaids the unpleasant task of carrying dirty bathwater down narrow, winding staircases. Unfortunately the hot water still had to be brought up by hand.

She enjoyed her soak and stepped, fragrant and clean, from the bathtub with, Jane informed her, an hour to get dressed for dinner. 'I don't intend to go down tonight, Jane. I have a sick headache and must retire to bed. I wish you to send a message to my mother apologising and telling her I shan't be joining her for dinner.'

Jane was immediately concerned. 'I'm not surprised you feel poorly, my lady. All that gallivanting about in the sunshine and without any luncheon — it was bound to make you ill. I shall send down for one of Cook's tisanes at once.'

'No, thank you. I just wish to sleep. I'm sure I'll be quite restored by morning. I was so looking forward to dining with the duke tonight, but he's here to stay, so there will be many more nights to spend in his company. With my sisters there to entertain him and his friend Lord Davenport at his side, I'm sure I won't be missed.' She felt a twinge of conscience at her falsehoods, but better to lie than risk an unpleasant confrontation with her guardian.

'That's untrue. I'm sure the evening won't be as entertaining without you there.' Jane slipped a cool cotton night-dress over Rosamond's head. 'There — you mustn't fret, my lady. You cannot help being unwell.'

Within a short space of time, Rosamond was safely tucked up in bed with the hangings pulled shut so she couldn't be seen by anyone who might step into her bedchamber. She instructed her maid to close the shutters and curtains as well, so the room was pleasantly cool and dark. She did occasionally suffer from a megrim and had decided that following her exact routine for a real headache would make her illness seem genuine.

Her apartment was at the rear of the house and overlooked the stables and paddocks; her sisters had chambers at the front close to the two master suites. Mama still occupied the rooms intended for the reigning duchess, and the duke was now in Papa's apartment. She hoped their proximity would not prove to be an unmitigated disaster.

The advantage of being in what might be considered an inferior position meant her apartment was isolated from the rest of her family and she was free to come and go without her mother being cognisant of her whereabouts. The disadvantage was that if she was reading in her parlour she couldn't hear the gong that was rung to send everyone to their chambers to change for dinner. Her tardiness was legendary and a constant source of irritation to Mama.

She was going to be ravenous by morning, as she could hardly ask for a supper tray when she was supposed to be languishing in bed with a sick headache. She wished now she'd gone in to eat at midday and not been dashing all over the park with her dog. Calli was not officially allowed in her apartment, but she often smuggled him in by the back stairs and none of the staff would dream of tittle-tattling about her misdemeanour.

She had never been less tired in her life and however much she plumped her pillows, she couldn't rest. She tried to push the image of a huge, furious dark-haired gentleman from her mind. Hiding in her apartment was only delaying retribution. Although she knew little about her adversary, one thing she was certain of — his threats were not idle ones. However, she was praying that by morning he would be more sanguine and her punishment would be less severe than a beating, although she couldn't think what his alternative retribution might be.

'Duchess, may I be permitted to compliment you on your ensemble?' Elliott bowed deeply and the small round lady dipped in a minimal curtsy. He turned his attention to the fluttering girls. 'Lady Amelia, I don't believe I've seen a more beautiful gown anywhere in London.' He stepped forward and inclined his head. She curtsied and he took her hand and raised it to his lips, although he drew the line at kissing her gloved fingers.

'Thank you, sir. My gowns are made for me in town, which is why they are in the first stare of fashion.'

He nodded at the younger two and they curtsied but seemed relieved not to be spoken to directly. He offered his arm to the dowager and with some reluctance she placed her plump fingers upon it. He drew her to one side. 'Madam, where is Lady Rosamond?'

'I'm sorry to inform you, sir, that my daughter is prostrate with a sick headache and will not be joining us tonight. However, Lady Amelia, my eldest daughter, is anticipating a private word with you before dinner.'

'Then she will be disappointed on that score, Duchess, as I have no reason to wish to speak to her alone.' Now or never — the dowager was already pursing her lips and preparing to deliver a severe set-down. 'A marriage will take place between Lady Rosamond and myself at the earliest opportunity. The sooner this matter is settled the better for all of us.' He glared at her, daring her to make an adverse comment on his choice. 'You will be delighted to hear, madam, that I've instructed workmen to prepare the Dower House for you. This will be ready for your occupation within a week. Lady Rosamond will no doubt decide whether her sisters are to remain here or join you in your new abode.'

The woman was speechless, which made a pleasant change for all concerned. Before she could voice her displeasure, Gibson announced that dinner was served and she had no option but to replace her hand on his arm and accompany him into the dining room.

He stopped so abruptly at the door of the chamber that her hand was torn from its place and her momentum carried her onwards. 'Good God! Why in heaven's name are we eating in this room? The table could seat more than fifty and we're but a small party.' He turned to Gibson. 'I refuse to eat in here. Have a table laid up in a smaller chamber.' The man had the temerity to hesitate. 'I gave you an instruction. I don't intend to ask a second time.'

The man recovered his composure and dinner was delayed for no more than a few minutes. Davenport accompanied Lady Amelia and they appeared to enjoy each other's company. He was aware, however, that she cast anxious looks in his direction every so often as if expecting him to disapprove. He must make an announcement before things became complicated.

He was about to tap his glass for silence when it occurred to him it might have been better if he had spoken to the lady in question before announcing to her family that she was to marry him. He had no doubt her headache was expedient — that she was hiding from her just desserts, and so only had herself to blame for being the last to know of her good fortune.

His lips curved as he recalled that he'd threatened to beat her. He'd never raised his hand to a child or a woman and had no intention of doing so now. But it would do her no harm to spend an anxious night before discovering he wasn't the monster she feared.

He cleared his throat and the five diners immediately fell silent. 'I have made my decision, and Lady Rosamond is to be my wife — ' Before he could complete his announcement, Lady Amelia jumped to her feet and her chair crashed noisily to the boards.

'I don't believe it. Why should you

wish to marry Rosamond? She's plain, unruly, and has no interest in becoming a duchess. In fact, she won't have you. She has told me often enough she intends to be a writer and be no man's wife.' She drew breath to continue her tirade but he'd heard more than enough.

He stood up slowly and spoke quietly but with great effect. His eyes bored into her. 'Enough, miss. You forget yourself. I won't be spoken to so disrespectfully at my own table. Go to your room at once. I'll deal with you in the morning.'

She didn't argue — no one did when he was angry — but turned and fled from the room, and her sobs could be heard as she ran away. He resumed his seat and continued his meal as if nothing unusual had taken place. He wasn't the only one relieved when the final cover was removed and the ladies could escape. No sooner had they gone than Davenport spoke his mind.

'That was poorly done, Bromley.

You've managed to alienate the entire family in the space of a few hours. God help you when Lady Rosamond hears second-hand that she's to be your bride.'

4

Rosamond had drawn back the bed curtains and was about to sneak out and find a book when her sitting room door crashed open. She dived under the covers and held her breath. There could only be one person who would burst into her private apartment like that — the duke had come to seek his revenge.

Then her bedchamber door flew open and Millie ran in and threw herself on the bed in hysterics. 'What is it? Millie, calm down. Take a deep breath and tell me what's wrong.' She gathered her sobbing sister into her arms and offered what comfort she could. Something disastrous had occurred to upset her normally sweet-tempered sibling.

Eventually the crying became gasps and her sister sat up. Before Rosamond could react, Millie launched herself at her and a fusillade of punches and scratches rocked her back against the headboard. Rosamond grabbed her sister's flailing arms and pinned them to her sides. 'For God's sake, Millie, what's wrong with you? Why are you attacking me?'

The look of hatred on Millie's face appalled her. 'How did you do it? You know I had set my heart on marrying him, and he would never have chosen you if you hadn't compromised yourself in some way.'

Whatever she had been expecting to be accused of, it was not this. 'Control yourself; you're speaking nonsense. You know my feelings on the subject of matrimony and they haven't changed one iota. What maggot has got into your brain? The duke has no more intention of marrying me than I have of marrying him.'

Her sister's expression softened somewhat. 'I don't understand at all. The duke announced at dinner just now that he has decided you are to be his bride.'

Rosamond thought it safe to release her sister's hands. 'Had he been drinking? Was he in his cups? The last time he spoke to me he was threatening to beat me. He is the reason I'm skulking up here and being obliged to miss my dinner. There must be some mistake; I am the very last person he would wish to marry.' She scrambled from the bed and rang the bell. 'I'll get dressed at once and go down and speak to him. I've no idea why he should wish to upset everyone in this way, but I'll find out.'

Millie blew her nose noisily on the sheet and then joined her on the carpet. 'What did you do to him? Why should he wish to beat you?'

'The man is an imbecile. He thought Sultan was bolting with me and attempted to remove me from the saddle.' She giggled inappropriately. 'Instead, I removed him from his saddle. Also, Sultan attacked him.'

'You cannot go downstairs — he is

already in a fearful rage with me. He might carry out his threat if you provoke him further.'

Jane bustled in, preventing further conversation. 'Are you feeling better, my lady? You certainly look more animated than before.'

'I am much recovered and would like a supper tray sent up for both of us.'

Her abigail curtsied but didn't comment on this strange request. 'I shall do so immediately, my lady. Do you wish to get dressed?'

'I think not, thank you. I'll put on my robe and my sister and I will eat in my sitting room.' She hesitated. Should she involve her maid in this muddle? 'Jane, what's going on downstairs? Have you heard anything about a disagreement over dinner?'

'My lady, it's not for me to pass on gossip, but downstairs everyone is saying that his grace is in a frightful temper and Lord Davenport is trying to placate him.' She fidgeted and refused to look her mistress in the face.

'Go on, Jane. What else is being said?'

'I beg your pardon, my lady, to be the bearer of such bad tidings, but his grace has decided he will marry none other than yourself.'

A wave of dizziness almost overwhelmed Rosamond, and she had never fainted in her life. She dug her fingernails into her palms and the sharp pain immediately restored her. 'This is absolutely intolerable. How dare the wretched man announce this to all and sundry without first speaking to me?' She threw her precious novel across the room and it smashed against the wall and fell in tatters to the floor. 'I wish to go downstairs. Jane, find me something to put on. I care not what it is. The first thing you lay hands on in my closet will do.'

Her sister edged round her. 'I beg your pardon for attacking you, dear sister, but please don't confront him when you're so cross. You can only make things worse. I realise now this wasn't your doing, but I fear there is nothing either of us can do. One of us must marry the duke, and if he won't have me, then it falls to you to save the family.'

'But you are desperate to become his duchess. Surely it would be far better for you to take this role than for me?'

'I have changed my mind. I couldn't live with a man who terrifies me. Much as I would like to be fabulously rich and married to a duke, this is not the duke I wish to marry. When you are his duchess you can open the townhouse and introduce me to another one — '

Despite her fury, Rosamond smiled at her sister's ingenuous remarks. 'Dearest, you're getting ahead of yourself. I have as little interest in marrying him as you do and have no wish to be the sacrificial lamb. And might I remind you, this is the only duke on offer. It might be years before another catch like him comes on the marriage market.' Millie was paying attention so she warmed to her theme. 'In fact, our duke is probably the most eligible bachelor in the country. He is prodigiously handsome and in his prime. For all his bluster, I would wager he would never carry out his threats. Will you not give him another chance? I'll go down directly and speak to him, explain my feelings and convince him he would be best suited with a more compliant bride.'

'Do you think so, Rosamond? You're right to point this out to me — I'll never have a better opportunity than this.' She sighed loudly and sniffed inelegantly. 'Although, sister, I don't believe he's the kind of gentleman to change his mind once he has made a decision. We mustn't forget he's a soldier; he will have been used to giving orders and expecting them to be instantly obeyed.'

'That's as may be, but for both our sakes I must try and convince him that he has chosen badly.' She grinned and pointed to the mangled book. 'I think I shall rant and rave and throw things at him, and convince him he is about to tie himself to a veritable termagant.'

'Oh, please don't do that. He might have you locked up in an asylum.'

'In which case, Millie dearest, he will have no option but to marry you — and when you're established as his wife you can insist that he has me released into your care.'

Jane deftly helped her into a demure long-sleeved gown, and Millie arranged her hair in a loose topknot. 'There — you look beautiful, Rosamond. Green of any shade is perfect on you. Quickly, put on your slippers. You must get downstairs before the gentlemen consume too much brandy.'

The thought of approaching an inebriated giant was almost too much for her, but she must make every effort to dissuade him from this path. She arrived in the hall, which was mysteriously empty of any waiting footmen.

She decided not to go through the grand drawing room but take the right-hand passageway which led directly to the dining room. The doors of this grand chamber were wide open and the room had obviously not been used tonight. Where was a footman when you needed him? Mama would no doubt have retired to her own apartment, and her younger sisters gone with her, so there was little danger in being confronted by one of them.

What she was going to do was outrageous, beyond the pale, totally unacceptable. Her mouth curved as she mentally listed all the ways her parent would describe her behaviour. She paused outside the room Papa had favoured as an informal dining room. She pressed her ear to the wood. Yes, definitely the sound of male voices within.

She hesitated. Did she wish to speak her piece in front of a witness? Would it not be better for her scandalous behaviour to remain a secret between the duke and herself? Then she reconsidered; the man she was about to confront might be less likely to roar at her if his friend was present.

She closed her eyes and sent up a quick prayer, as she rather thought divine intervention would be the only thing that could rectify the situation. Should she knock? No, this was her home and she was free to go anywhere she wished without the necessity of announcing herself.

The doors opened inwards and she pushed them with more force than was sensible. They swung open and smashed against the walls. The duke and Davenport had been talking quietly by the open windows at the far end of the room, and her dramatic entrance caused Davenport to throw his brandy over his friend. This was not received with any degree of equanimity.

'What in God's name are you thinking of, Lady Rosamond? Was it your intention to cause me further injury?'

Oh dear, this was not a propitious start. 'I do beg your pardon. I didn't mean to startle you both.' She curtsied briefly and turned her attention to the gentleman who was glaring at her in a most unpleasant way.

'I have come to rectify a misunderstanding, sir. For some reason you announced that I am to be your wife, which is quite incorrect. I have absolutely no intention of marrying you, nor anyone else, in the foreseeable future.' She returned his glare with one of her own. 'My sister will make you a perfect bride. I'm considered slightly unhinged by all who know me.'

They were both staring at her as if she was conversing in a foreign tongue. Now was the time to reinforce her position by doing something outrageous. There was a dish of nuts and another of ripe peaches — which should she throw first? Before either gentleman could react, she jumped forward and hurled the fruit, including the silver bowl, at the duke. His reflexes were superb, but he was able only to prevent the dish from braining him, the soft peaches splattering satisfactorily all over his chest.

He was moving towards her when she met him with a barrage of nuts. She looked around for something else to throw and her eyes settled on the decanter of port. She snatched it up and was taking aim when he reached her. 'No, my lady, I think not. You're like to kill someone with a glass container.'

Instead of being furious he was laughing at her; a strange strangled sound was coming from the far end of the room and she glanced up to see Lord Davenport collapsed in a heap, rocking from side to side with laughter.

She lashed out at the duke and struggled to remove her wrists from his iron grip. 'Let me go. I told you, I'm dangerously deranged. I should be locked away immediately.'

'What you should be, my love, is soundly spanked, and I'm sorely tempted to do so right now.'

She no longer cared what he did, as for some reason he hadn't been repelled by her disgraceful behaviour. She looked at him and there was definitely a decided glint in his eye. There was nothing she could do to prevent him, so she might as well continue to annoy him. 'Do you wish to administer the spanking, your grace, before or after you have removed the squashed peaches from your evening coat?' She smiled sweetly and nodded at his dishevelment. 'This is a new gown, sir, and I have no wish to have it spoiled by soft fruit.'

He smiled down at her and something most peculiar happened to her insides. 'I have had brandy, peaches and nuts thrown over me, but you are to remain pristine? I think not, my dear.'

Before she could protest he swept her into the air and crushed her against his disgusting jacket, then rolled her from side to side to make sure she was liberally coated in the muck. Having her breasts flattened was decidedly unpleasant but she was prepared to suffer the indignity as this was preferable to being put across his knee. Then everything changed and a searing pain in her right shoulder caused her to cry out.

Instantly he held her away and his expression changed from amusement to horror. 'My God, what have I done? No, don't touch your shoulder, sweetheart; you cannot remove the pin just yet.' He called over his shoulder to his friend, who was no longer laughing. 'Davenport, your stock, if you please. I've managed to impale Lady Rosamond with my stock pin. I fear it might have nicked a vein.'

Rosamond glanced down and was shocked to see blood oozing from around the diamond pin sticking out of her shoulder. How had the duke's pin become embedded in her? Why couldn't she pull it out?

'Please, I would much prefer you pulled it out as it is rather painful.' He was supporting her with one arm whilst holding the pin steady with the other hand. Davenport appeared beside them with a folded white cloth.

'Sweetheart, lean your weight against me, and when you're settled I'll remove the pin. Davenport will apply pressure to the wound. Are you ready?'

'I am. I don't feel quite well, sir. I believe I might be going to faint.' Darkness enveloped her.

★ ★ ★

'Thank God; this will be easier if she's unconscious. I'll place her on the table before you do it.' Elliott stretched the girl out there on the polished surface whilst his friend kept the pressure on her shoulder. 'Quickly, man, get the damn thing out. I want to see how bad it is.' The pin slid from the wound but to his profound relief a gush of gore didn't follow. 'Keep the pad on the puncture whilst I remove my neck cloth. I can secure the dressing using that.'

By the time he'd finished, the patient was stirring and both he and Davenport were liberally covered with her blood, but the wound was no longer bleeding and the danger was over. He scooped her up and headed for the doors. 'I don't think we need a quack, Davenport, but I need to get her to bed. She's had more than enough excitement for today.'

'What are you doing? Where am I going? Put me down, please. You're making a spectacle of me.' Her voice was quiet but perfectly lucid.

'Remain still, my dear. You've lost a deal of blood and most of it's on me and Davenport. The injury is not as bad as I'd first feared; if you drink a jug of watered wine before you retire I guarantee you will be fully recovered in the morning.'

'I don't drink wine — it doesn't agree with me, sir — but I quite like lemonade.' A small hand reached out and casually flicked a lump of fruit from his lapel. 'I believe that we could say we have both received our just deserts.'

'You, my dear, are a baggage, but I find the more I see of you the better I like you.' She stirred against him. 'No, little one, remain still. You'll disturb the dressing if you wriggle.'

'I'll not marry you. You cannot make me. We are as unsuited as any couple in the kingdom — I believe that we might kill each other if we're thrust together in that way. Marry my sister. I promise you it would be better for both of us.'

A nervous footman had led him to the far side of the house and halted outside a door. 'This is Lady Rosamond's apartment, your grace.'

Elliott kicked it open and strode through to be met by two maidservants. 'Your mistress has injured her shoulder. I have dealt with it and she will be perfectly well in the morning. Make sure the dressing remains in place and that she drinks at least a pint of lemonade before she sleeps.'

Both girls appeared struck dumb. They pointed to the bedchamber and he walked through and gently placed her in the centre of the bed. 'One of you stay up with her. If she develops a fever, send for me immediately.' He leant down and spoke so softly he could not be overheard. 'I have made up my mind. I knew the moment I set eyes on you that you would make me the perfect wife. Accept the inevitable, my love. I won't change my mind.'

He straightened and left the girls to their task, puzzled that they hadn't done more than curtsy and nod. Were they so in awe of him that they had been incapable of speech? Only as he was returning to his apartment did he understand why the maids hadn't spoken. It wasn't awe but astonishment that had prevented them from uttering. He was covered in blood, peaches and cognac — he looked ridiculous.

He heard a clock strike somewhere close by. How could it only be eight o'clock when so much had happened? He would change into his riding gear and persuade his friend to ride with him. Rosamond was right to have reservations; he'd known her but a few hours and already had been pushed from his saddle, savaged by her horse and bombarded with fruit and nuts. And she had received what might have been a life-threatening injury at his hands.

Was he wrong to insist she marry him when she so clearly disliked the idea? He had to marry one of the girls, and damn quickly too. Amelia would definitely make a more biddable wife, and she was a diamond of the first water — should he reconsider his choice?

He had obtained four special licences, one for each prospective bride, so he could get married tomorrow if he so wished. He smiled as he recalled the astonishment of the clerk when he'd made his unprecedented request. When he'd explained his predicament the matter had been dealt with without further enquiry. He had given his word he would destroy the unwanted papers after he'd made his choice. When he had changed he carefully removed three of the documents and set light to them in the empty grate.

5

Rosamond slept soundly despite her injury and woke fully restored, eager to leave her bed at once. 'Jane, please put out my habit; I intend to take Sultan out as usual. You've removed the dressing and seen for yourself the puncture wound is almost healed and no longer even needs a bandage.'

'My lady, I'm sure his grace wouldn't approve of you riding this morning — '

'Fiddlesticks to that! I shall do as I please for as long as I can. I don't answer to him at the moment.' A delicious warmth enveloped her as she recalled his whispered words the previous evening. For the first time in her life she had been put ahead of her sisters. The duke didn't want to marry Millie; he wanted to make her his wife.

For all his shortcomings, and they

were legion, she was beginning to consider him in a different light. He might be dictatorial, over-large and over-loud, but last night he had shown a softer side to his character and she could not fault his treatment of her.

Would it be so very bad to be the one to save the family? Perhaps if he would agree to a marriage in name only — a convenient arrangement to allow him to access funds, being his duchess would not be so very bad.

'I'm perfectly well, Jane. My shoulder doesn't even hurt. I suppose my evening gown is quite ruined?'

'It is, my lady, but I can remove the bodice and the skirt can be reused. I believe there's a length of silk in a slightly darker colour that would work splendidly.'

'Then I'll leave it to you. I'm sure the gown will be perfectly lovely when you've finished. As far as I'm concerned, I can't see the point in spending hundreds of guineas on a gown made in London when one made right here is perfectly satisfactory.'

She was aware that the footmen she passed bowed to her this morning. Word of her imminent elevation must have spread around the house — did this mean she was no longer in a position to refuse the duke? She smiled as she left the house; until she'd received a formal offer from him she wasn't his betrothed and would continue to behave as she always did. She was still annoyed that he hadn't spoken to her before making his announcement, which showed a remarkable lack of tact on his part.

The stable yard was busy as usual, but when she looked in Sultan's box it was empty. Her dog greeted her enthusiastically but there was no sign of her horse. This was strange. Although he was turned out overnight, a groom always fetched him from the field first thing so she could ride. Albert was nowhere in sight, but no doubt someone else could be sent to collect her stallion. Was she imagining it, or were the grooms avoiding looking in her direction? She wasn't used to being ignored.

'Where is my horse? Fetch him at once; I wish to ride immediately.' She spoke loudly, addressing the command to anyone in the vicinity. The stable yard fell silent. Not a bucket banged or a barrow creaked, and still no one spoke to her. Then Albert appeared, looking decidedly shifty.

'I beg your pardon, my lady, but . . . but . . . his grace has given instructions with regard to your stallion. He is no longer available for you but is to be kept for his personal use in future. I've saddled Bruno. Shall I bring him out for you?'

For a moment she was unable to answer; her fury held her mute. She recovered sufficiently to speak briefly. 'No, I'll make my own arrangements.' What he made of her cryptic comment she'd no idea, and cared less. She stalked from the yard looking neither right nor left, and once through the archway gathered her skirt and raced to the paddock.

Sultan was trotting back and forth along the fence, whinnying anxiously. 'I know — it's not fair, and I don't intend to follow orders.' She climbed onto the fence and threw her arms around his neck. 'I can't ask to have you saddled, Sultan. Any groom who disobeyed a direct instruction would be dismissed. However, that wretched man will not stop us going out.'

She grabbed a handful of his wiry mane and dropped astride the massive horse. Fortunately the breeches she was wearing underneath her skirt made riding bareback possible. At least she would save herself from the further disgrace of showing an unseemly amount of leg. She adjusted the voluminous skirt of her riding habit and settled herself more comfortably.

This was not the first time she'd ridden him like this; as a young girl the two of them had frequently galloped all over the park before anyone was awake.

This was, however, the first time she'd attempted to ride him with no tack at all, not even a halter rope to guide him.

'Come along, Sultan. If we're to stay together then you must become accustomed to this unusual experience.' She leant forward and stroked his massive shoulder. 'You won't let me down. I trust you implicitly.'

There was only one way out of the paddock that wouldn't lead her past the stable yard, and that was over the fence. She prayed her ability to stay aboard without a saddle hadn't deserted her. That her horse could clear the obstacle she had no doubt; they frequently jumped hedges that were far wider and taller than the fence.

She squeezed gently with her knees and guided him by pulling his mane in the direction she wished to go. He eased smoothly into a collected canter and she circled the paddock, gradually urging him faster until they were racing towards the fence. She tipped slightly forward and lowered her hands. The magnificent animal soared into the air, clearing the jump by a yard or more.

She steadied him and he settled back into a rhythmic, controlled pace. She released her breath with a hiss — she could ride him safely without even a bridle, but until this moment she hadn't been absolutely certain. Now she could relax and enjoy her customary morning outing, and with any luck she could return him to his paddock without anyone being aware she'd taken him. For a second she was apprehensive. If the duke got wind of her excursion he wouldn't be pleased — in fact, she was pretty sure he would be incandescent with fury.

She pushed these unpleasant thoughts away. It was far too late to repine. Whatever transpired on her return, this morning she was going to enjoy riding her horse in the glorious early morning sunshine.

★   ★   ★

Elliott slept late, which was unusual for him, and was roused by the rattling of the curtains and the shuffling footsteps of his valet. He stretched and yawned and sprung out of bed. His man greeted him politely and continued to lay out his garments. The fact that his master slept buck naked was something he'd become accustomed to.

'I apologise for the state of my evening rig, Jenkins. A mishap with a bowl of fruit. The blood on my shirt was from Lady Rosamond. No doubt you've already heard all about it below stairs.'

'An accident with your pin, your grace, but not serious. Your shirt is beyond recovery, but your jacket will be as good as new by this evening.'

Elliott wandered towards the open window, eager for his first morning view of the land he was now lord and master of. The park was magnificent — no fussy ornamental gardens to spoil the view across the rolling grass and imposing trees. The glint of water on the horizon added to the charm of the vista. Capability Brown had been employed to transform these grounds, and an excellent job he had done too.

He was about to turn away when something caught his eye. Forgetting he was without clothes, he leaned out of the window to get a better view. God's teeth! Surely not — ? His heart hammered and the hair on the back of his neck prickled. That idiot girl had taken her horse and was galloping him across the park with nothing more to guide her than her hand on his neck.

He spun and shouted at Jenkins. 'My clothes! No time to shave; I need to be elsewhere immediately.' He was dressed and pulling on his boots in minutes, and left his apartment at a run. He jumped the last four steps, causing an unfortunate footman to drop the tray of silverware he was carrying. The resulting clatter brought several minions into the hall, but Elliott ignored them and continued his headlong dash to the side door.

He roared as he approached the archway for his horse to be brought out. His massive bay gelding was barely out of his box when he skidded up beside him. He snatched the halter rope from the groom, rested his left hand on the animal's withers and vaulted onto his back. Stable boys threw themselves sideways to avoid being trampled as he thundered out of the yard and galloped after the girl on the stallion.

As he crouched low he prayed Rosamond would be able to stay on the back of her horse. If she fell at the speed she was going she would break her neck as the marquis had done before her. This time he had no intention of trying to stop the stallion — in fact, he didn't actually know why he'd raced after her in this ridiculous way. There was something about this girl that brought out a protective streak in him he hadn't known he possessed. He wanted to cherish her, take care of her, keep her safe from her madcap ventures.

He checked his horse and they settled into a comfortable canter as he guided the gelding diagonally across the acres of green parkland on a course he hoped would bring him to a point his quarry would cross. The land undulated and he reached the highest point upon which was built a Greek folly. To his surprise both fodder and water had been left inside the artificial ruins for the horses, as well as a table, two chairs and a picnic hamper for the humans.

Excellent — this was obviously a regular haunt of the girl. He slid to the ground and dropped the halter rope in front of his horse in the hope the beast would treat it in the same way he would his reins. The water was sweet and clean; some unfortunate stable boy must have trekked out here recently to replenish the buckets.

The sun was warm even this early in the day, and he moved into the shade of the folly to wait for Rosamond. He saw her emerge from the woods. His chest squeezed and his mouth went dry.

Ahead of the girl was an enormous hedge — surely she wasn't going to try and jump that bareback? He'd never seen a woman ride as well as she did. If he were honest, she was most definitely the most accomplished rider of either sex that he knew.

She steadied the stallion and they approached the jump at a gallop. He held his breath as she rose into the air and cleared the obstacle easily, to land impeccably yards from the hedge and continue her wild ride up the slope. He hadn't deliberately hidden his mount from her view, but now he intentionally moved into the shadow of the folly and watched her bring her magnificent mount back to a collected canter and then to a walk.

★ ★ ★

Rosamond had never enjoyed a ride as much as she had today. The added danger of being both astride and bareback was exactly what she liked.

She abhorred the humdrum, and wanted every day to be an adventure of some sort and not a tedious repetition of the day before.

'We'll walk the last half a mile, Sultan. Then you'll be cool enough to drink when we arrive at the folly. I hope someone has had the forethought to bring out the food and water today, as they might have thought I wouldn't come this far on Bruno.' Her horse snorted and his ears moved back and forth as if he was listening to her. Then his muscles bunched and his ears pricked. 'What is it? Have you heard something?'

They were almost at the folly as she spoke, and to her horror the very man she wished to avoid stepped out. Before she could gather her wits and turn her horse he was beside her, his arm a band of steel around her waist, making escape impossible. Without a word he removed her from Sultan's back and tossed her over his shoulder as if she was a sack of potatoes, and then he marched into the folly.

Her ability to speak returned, as did her wish to be released. 'Put me down, you brute. I will not be manhandled in this way.' Each phrase was accompanied by a hefty kick. Her boots connected satisfactorily with solid flesh and she renewed her struggles to escape.

'I warn you, Rosamond, if you kick me again I will respond. I guarantee you will find yourself unable to sit comfortably for at least a week if I do.' She froze mid-kick. She had no doubt whatsoever that he would carry out his threat. He tipped her unceremoniously to the ground and her legs crumpled beneath her. He made no attempt to pick her up or offer her any assistance or sympathy. What was the point in fighting? He would win every battle because he had the law on his side, as well as being the size of a giant.

Defeated, she drew up her knees, folded her arms around them and dropped her head. The folly had been her favourite place, but now even that had been spoiled by this bully. Tears seeped through her closed fingers and she swallowed an unwanted sob. He was tending to the horses; they were snuffling and shifting in their eagerness to drink. A chair scraped on the marble floor and there was the unmistakable sound of the picnic basket being unfastened.

An appetising aroma of freshly baked bread filled her nostrils and her stomach gurgled in response. Was she to sit here in ignominy whilst he devoured the contents of *her* hamper?

'Do you intend to sit sulking there indefinitely, my dear?' There was an infuriating rattle and further tantalising smells drifted down to her. 'We have strawberry conserve, a fine strong cheese, butter — oh, and I do believe there is the best part of a fine plum cake to go with the delicious lemonade.'

Her head shot up and she wanted to throw something hard and heavy at his head. He met her vitriolic stare with a quizzical eyebrow and a smile played around his lips. Her hands were now flat on the ground and her questing fingers fastened on something suitable.

'I think not, sweetheart. Far better to join me for this picnic than the alternative, don't you think?' His expression was bland but the warning in his eyes was unmistakable.

She released the shard of stone and sprung to her feet. 'This is *my* place — where Papa and I came every morning in the summer. Now you have ruined it. You've driven him away. He's gone forever now.' She gulped and turned her back to hide her misery.

'Sweetheart, don't cry. I can't bear to see you distressed.' This time his hold was gentle and he turned her so she could rest her head on his shoulder whilst he stroked her back and she cried as if her heart would break. Eventually the storm was over and she sniffed loudly. 'Here, little one, use this — dry your eyes and come and sit down with me. We need to talk.'

She blew her nose noisily and was tempted to hand him back the disgusting cloth but instead she pushed it up her sleeve. 'This is all such a dreadful muddle. Nothing has gone right at Hathersage since Charles died three years ago.' His arm was still around her waist and she was too dispirited to protest. He guided her to the table and she was glad to be seated, as her legs still felt as if they belonged to someone else.

'Here, bread and jam and lemonade — don't talk until you've consumed it all.'

He was right. By the time she'd demolished three slices of bread and jam, drunk most of the lemonade and eaten a substantial portion of the plum cake, she was feeling more herself. She brushed the crumbs from her lap and wiped her lips on a napkin provided in the picnic hamper. He had been watching her for the past ten minutes, his long booted legs stretched out and crossed at the ankles, his arms folded across his chest, the picture of complete relaxation and control.

'You will be relieved to know, sir, that I'm replete. I apologise for eating so much, but I hadn't eaten since yesterday morning.' She turned her chair away from the table and nodded in his direction. 'I might have had supper last night if I hadn't been previously injured by someone.'

His demeanour changed and he swung round to face her. 'You are right to remind me, my dear. What I did was unforgivable. I do most humbly apologise for hurting you.' He smiled wryly. 'However, in my defence I will say that I had just been bombarded with fruit and nuts and was merely attempting to return the favour.'

'And I tender my apologies for behaving like a lunatic.' She paused, and from nowhere came a desire to explain the whole to him. 'Millie and I hoped you would be given such a disgust of me you would reconsider your decision and marry her instead.

She did point out that you might have me incarcerated in an asylum, but I was prepared to take that risk.'

The words were said in jest but he looked so horrified she realised he had misunderstood her intention. Without thinking she reached out and patted his hands. 'No, sir, neither of us truly thought my behaviour would change anything. I can assure you, even marriage to you is preferable to being considered a dangerous lunatic.'

His reaction was so unexpected she almost fell from the chair. He threw his head back and roared with laughter. The sound was infectious and soon she was giggling along with him. Sometime later he mopped his eyes and shook his head as if mystified by what had happened.

'Lady Rosamond, I believe you to be the only young lady in the nation who would have the courage to speak to me like that. Tell me, exactly how unpleasant do you consider marrying me to be?'

'Obviously not as bad as a lunatic asylum, but . . . ' This was no longer amusing; he was staring at her too intently. She must answer honestly if she wished to make him understand.

6

Rosamond closed her eyes so she could marshal her thoughts without him staring into her soul. Keeping her head lowered, she began her explanation. 'My father knew I had no interest in marriage; that my heart's desire lay in becoming a published novelist. My trust fund was set up in such a way that on my twenty-fifth anniversary the money becomes mine. I intended to have my own establishment.

'When my brother died everything changed. Believe it or not, Mama was slim and pretty then, but since his death she has lost interest in her appearance and eats nothing but marchpane and cakes. Then when Papa was afflicted he changed his will so whoever inherited the title would be obliged to marry one of us. He did this to ensure the title and estates would pass eventually to a close family member through the female side.'

'Yes, that makes perfect sense to me. However, my dear, I'm still waiting to hear why you are so against becoming my bride.'

'I would have thought that was obvious, sir. Not only do I have no interest in matrimony or producing annual offspring, but I neither like nor respect you. I cannot think of anyone less well suited to the state of matrimony.' She was warming to his theme and looked directly at him.

He nodded gravely. 'It's invigorating to be so roundly dismissed.' He captured her waving hands. 'Would you care to enter a wager with me?'

'I don't approve of gambling.'

'In which case, I'll call it a challenge. Indeed, everything about you is a challenge to me. And I never could resist one — and let that be a warning, my dear, as I always achieve my goals.'

Having her hands restrained beneath his calloused palms was strangely disturbing. She attempted to pull away but was unable to. 'What is this challenge? I am becoming bored with this conversation and wish to return home.'

'My challenge is to change your mind about marriage in general and marriage to me in particular. Do you think I can do it?'

Something fluttered inside her. He was offering her a lifeline. If she agreed to his proposition it would give her several valuable months to convince him he would be better off with Millie. 'No, I am sure that you can't. However, I'm prepared to let you try.' She tried a second time to remove her hands. 'Let us say that if after six months I'm still not agreeable, you will agree to marry my sister.'

His eyes blazed. 'You have quite misunderstood the matter, Lady Rosamond. You will marry me tomorrow. My challenge is to persuade you that you wish to be my true wife.'

This time she pulled her hands with

such force he had to let it go. She was on her feet and backing away from him, unable to accept his statement. 'I will marry you because I have no choice, but I vow I will never willingly allow you in my bed. If you wish to secure the title you must do so by force.'

Instead of being enraged by her impertinence, he slowly stood up and closed the distance between them in one stride. He stood so close his breath mingled with hers. She raised her hand, intending to push him away, but when it touched his chest and his heart was thundering beneath her fingers, there was something between them. She couldn't move; she was held captive by some unknown force greater than her. She raised her head and a wave of heat engulfed her.

He gathered her, unresisting, into his embrace. 'Exactly so, my love. We have already established a deep connection.' He could have taken advantage of the situation and made love to her, but he just cradled her gently and murmured into her hair. 'No doubt we'll fight like cat and dog, but I promise you our union won't be dull. I have given you my word that you'll have six months to sleep alone.' His proximity was unsettling her in a way she wasn't sure she liked. 'However, my bedchamber door will always be unlocked should you wish to join me before then.'

She jerked backwards. 'Never. I wish you to give me your word you won't force me into your bed at any time. I really couldn't marry you if I truly believed that you'd do such a dreadful thing.'

'I'm saddened that you consider me so low a person — no gentleman would ever force his attentions upon a lady, even one that is his wife.'

'In which case, reluctantly, I will become your duchess.' Some imp of mischief made her continue. 'I don't believe you've actually asked me to marry you. That is very ungallant, I must say.'

His snort of disgust made her giggle.

She stood, ankles together and hands demurely held in front of her, and waited to see how he would handle this.

He lunged forward dramatically, grabbed both her hands and fell to one knee. 'My darling Rosamond, will you make me the happiest of men? Will you accept my hand in matrimony?'

'Thank you, kind sir. I am deeply honoured by your request.' She forced her quivering lips into a look of disapproval as if she were about to refuse, and was delighted to see a momentary flicker of doubt in his eyes. 'I am happy to accept your offer, although I think you're making the most appalling error in choosing me and not my sister.'

He rose and kissed her knuckles. 'As I've said before, and no doubt will repeat many times in the future, you are a baggage and sorely in need of restraint.'

'I don't disagree, sir, but you have only yourself to blame if you regret this union at a later date.' She nodded sagely.

'I will collect our mounts whilst you repack the picnic hamper.' This seemed a sensible suggestion so she didn't feel the need to argue. Everything was tidy when he strolled back in. His nonchalant air left her unprepared for his attack.

'You won't ride Sultan again until I give you leave — not bareback, not saddled. Is that quite clear?'

She swallowed her impertinent reply. He was in no mood for prevarication on her part. She curtsied politely. 'I understand, your grace, and will do as you instruct.' She should have left it there, but her sense of outrage at his decision prompted her to speak unwisely. 'I take it this punishment is because I tipped you from your saddle yesterday? If you had not tried to do the same to me — '

'Hold your tongue. My decisions are not open to debate. The sooner you understand that, my lady, the better we shall deal together.'

In stony silence she turned her back

to him and offered her bent leg so he could toss her onto her horse. Only then did she notice that he, too, had ridden bareback and without a bridle. Ignoring good manners and common sense, she kicked the stallion into a flat gallop, leaving her tormentor to follow if he wished. If this were to be the last ride, then she was going to make it something to remember.

*   *   *

Elliott watched her vanish but made no attempt to follow her. He was forced to admit he was more likely to come to grief in a mad race over the countryside than she was. He frowned. Was he wrong to marry Rosamond when she was so reluctant?

Perhaps such a hasty ceremony wasn't necessary — after all, the estate had been without funds for more than a year, so another week or two could hardly matter. Decision made, he vaulted on his horse and made a leisurely return to Hathersage Hall. Neither groom nor stable boy was visible in the yard. He grinned. They would be making themselves scarce until he left them in peace to get on with their tasks.

Albert, braver than the rest, approached him, his face anxious. 'Lady Rosamond hasn't returned. Should I send out a search party?'

'No, she'll be back eventually. I hold no one responsible for what happened, and I'm certain there will not be a repeat of this morning's escapade. I'll ride Sultan in future and Lady Rosamond must select a different mount.'

There was still no evidence that the other ladies of the house were up. No doubt they, too, were avoiding him, but that didn't explain the absence of his friend, who was normally up with the lark. He spoke to one of the footmen on duty in the hall. 'Is Lord Davenport down?'

'Lord Davenport is in the breakfast

parlour, your grace. Would you like me to show you the whereabouts of this chamber?'

Elliott shook his head. Once he was properly established he would speak to Gibson about having so many active young men trapped in a meaningless occupation all day. He doubted if either of the footmen opened and shut doors more than half a dozen times between them. They wouldn't be dismissed, of course, so he must devise an occupation for them that wouldn't be considered beneath their dignity but was less tedious.

He was smiling when he eventually discovered the breakfast parlour; he'd been down several corridors and opened countless doors without success before reaching his destination. At least he had sensible employment for the two young men — for the next few days he would use them to guide him around his new property. No doubt Davenport could do with assistance also.

'Good morning, Bromley. Have you

broken your fast? Your butler informed me that you and Lady Rosamond were riding together. Is she to join us?'

'We had a picnic meal at the folly so I'm here for coffee, not sustenance.' He waved away the lurking footmen and they vanished through a hidden door in the panelling. He poured himself a cup of the aromatic brew he preferred to tea and gulped it down, then refilled his cup before joining his friend at the table. 'Lady Rosamond is still careering about the park on her magnificent horse. As this will be the last time she rides him until I give her leave, I doubt she'll be back until much later.'

'That's a bit harsh, Bromley. Are you punishing her for your mistakes?'

Elliott gritted his teeth and forced himself to take a soothing mouthful of coffee before risking an answer. 'Strangely enough, that's exactly what she accused me of. Perhaps there's some truth in what you say, but my order remains in place for the moment.' His annoyance at being found out so easily faded. 'I'll magnanimously rescind my instructions in a day or two. It will do her no harm to be forced to do as she's told for once in her life. Although overlooked by her mother, during the old duke's lifetime she was indulged and spoilt by him.' He swallowed the remainder of his drink and reached for the silver coffee pot to replenish it. 'Her inheritance is not part of the estate. In fact, it remains hers alone even after marriage. She intended to remain a spinster in her own establishment and write romantic novels. Have you ever heard of such a thing?'

Davenport chuckled. 'I haven't, but it sounds an excellent idea to me. Why should a girl give up everything when she marries? Seems very unfair.' He dropped his cutlery with a clatter. 'Mind you, I don't know how most of my cronies would stay afloat if it weren't for the money they've gained from their wives.' He stood up and patted Elliott on the shoulder. 'I should stamp out any idea of novel-writing, if I were you. She might expect you to behave like a hero. Now tell me, have you reconciled Lady Rosamond to her fate?'

'Reconciled? I think not, but she has agreed to marry me. It was my intention to hold the ceremony tomorrow and I have already sent word to the rector, but I've reconsidered that. I no longer wish to be married in a havy cavy way, but with all the pomp and ceremony that befits my elevated station.'

'That could work either way, my friend. Allowing Lady Rosamond more time to dwell on what she's committing herself to might not be the best notion in the circumstances. I intend to ride around your magnificent estate. No doubt you have business matters to attend to.'

'The estate manager is coming soon, and then I must make my peace with the duchess and discuss my revised plans for my nuptials.'

Davenport turned at the door. 'Might it not be better to discuss these with your future wife rather than her appalling mother?'

For a moment Elliott wished to hurl something after his friend. Then he smiled. He had been only a day as the head of this vast establishment and already he was behaving quite out of character. He had been renowned for his cool head and decisive action under fire, yet in the space of a few hours he was behaving as badly as the volatile young woman he had decided to marry. Could meeting her have changed him so completely?

★ ★ ★

Rosamond half-expected the duke to follow her and wasn't sure if she was relieved or disappointed that he didn't. She no longer wished to thunder about the countryside risking her neck, but she didn't want to go back just yet, so decided to spend an hour or two in the woods.

Under the pale green canopy the

path seemed magical, as if there might indeed be fairies shimmering somewhere under leaves. She wished she had a fairy godmother who could turn the clock back three years so she could prevent her brother taking that final, fatal ride. She wiped her eyes on her gloves and swallowed the lump in her throat. Even if Charles was still alive, Papa would still be dead and her brother would be head of the household instead of a dictatorial ex-soldier.

'Good grief! Perhaps fate hasn't been as unkind as I thought to this family. Charles would have made a dismal custodian. His only interests were gambling, drinking and making ridiculous wagers with his cronies.' She spoke her words aloud and Sultan nodded and flicked his ears, obviously agreeing with her.

Apart from the fact that she was obliged to marry the wretched man, things were not so bleak as she supposed. For all his arrogance, the duke would run Hathersage as well as her father had — indeed, he might even make a better fist of it.

'Shall we go back? I don't know about you, old fellow, but I'm hot and uncomfortable and wish to wash and change into a muslin gown.'

When she handed over her horse to Albert she smiled sadly. 'I'm not to ride him again. I expect the duke has told you so.'

'Yes, my lady. He explained it all. However, he said you are free to ride any other horse in the stable.'

For a moment she didn't take his meaning. 'Any animal? Are you quite sure?' Albert nodded gleefully. 'Then tomorrow morning I'll take his gelding. I doubt the animal will take a side saddle, so I'll ride astride.'

'You'll be wanting to go at first light, I reckon, my lady. I'll have him waiting at six.'

'Thank you, Albert. I'll be here.' She ran to the house, bubbling with excitement. Her tormentor would be hopping mad but be able to do nothing

114

about it. He had given her permission to ride his horse even though she was certain that hadn't been his intention.

As usual she took the back stairs, which brought her out in the spacious passageway opposite her apartment door. She burst into her parlour, eager to complete her ablutions and seek out her sisters to gauge their reaction to her sudden elevation. Mama would have a great deal to say on the subject, none of it complimentary to either herself or her future husband, but she hoped to avoid this confrontation for as long as possible.

'Jane, I've agreed to marry him. Nothing I could say or do would change his mind. I must dress to impress. What do you suggest?'

'Your bath is all but cold, my lady. Shall I send for fresh hot water?'

Rosamond shook her head. 'A cold bath is exactly what I need. I'll wash my hair as well. I'm quite sure I still have peach pulp embedded in it.'

'As to your gown, my lady, I know

exactly what you should wear. Do you recall the Indian cotton you liked so much? The material has gold thread woven through the green. It will perfectly complement your eyes and bring out the shine in your hair.'

There was no necessity to hurry as, despite being out of the house for almost three hours, it was still early and her siblings and mama would not descend from their chambers until noon. This gave her ample time for her hair to dry if she sat with it loose on a sunny window seat.

When she was finally ready, she gazed in amazement at her reflection in the full-length glass. 'You have worked a miracle, Jane. I've never looked so well.'

'Indeed, my lady, I've never seen you so animated. Your eyes are sparkling and your hair has never been so glossy.' Her maid shook out an imaginary crease from the skirt of the beautiful gown. 'You look every inch a duchess, my lady, and will be a perfect match for his grace.' The young woman blushed and curtsied. 'I beg your pardon, my lady, for speaking out of turn.'

'Please continue to talk to me as you have always have, Jane. I value your advice and friendship.' Rosamond grinned. 'Mind you, it might be better if you're as formal as possible when the duke is present.'

She had no need to take a reticule, put on a ridiculous bonnet or wear gloves, as she was not receiving visitors or intending to make morning calls. As she was descending the magnificent marble staircase, the duke strode across the tiles. She hesitated, not sure if she should retreat or advance. They hadn't parted on the best of terms.

He made the decision for her. 'My dear, allow me to say that you look quite enchanting dithering about on the stairs, but there are matters we need to discuss before we approach the dragon in her den. Would you care to join me in my study?'

7

'Do I have a choice?' He solemnly shook his head. 'In which case, sir, I shall be delighted to join you.' Rosamond skipped down the remaining stairs and curtsied to the tall, dark man, who was unaccountably looking rather pleased with himself. 'After all, it's not as though we are at daggers drawn, are we?'

He smiled and offered his arm. 'Come along, my dear. I don't have time to stand about bandying words with you.'

When they reached the door she hesitated, reluctant to enter a room she'd not entered since her father had died. Before she could explain, he walked past as if he hadn't intended to use that room. 'Do you have a destination in mind? This direction leads to a multitude of ante-rooms and various storerooms.' She glanced up and met his smiling gaze. 'If we reverse our steps and take the left-hand turn, that leads directly to the library.'

'Excellent. To the library we shall go. I'm in imminent danger of becoming hopelessly lost in this barracks of a place. I had intended to designate one of the redundant footmen in the hall to act as my guide, but they have mysteriously vanished.'

'Of course they have. They have other duties and only remain in the hall until everyone is down. They would be out of their minds with boredom otherwise.'

'If I'm to be denied my guide, I'll be forced to wander the long, empty corridors alone until eventually found half-starved.'

He was being ridiculous and absolutely irresistible. 'There isn't a building large enough for your voice not to be heard when you roar for attention.'

'Have you no respect for your future husband? I am marrying a veritable shrew.' He pulled her closer and squeezed her hand. 'Are you familiar with *The Taming of the Shrew* by William Shakespeare?' She nodded, knowing in which direction his thoughts were flowing. 'Then, my dearest love, be prepared for your come-uppance.'

Why did he lard his conversation with false endearments? Did he hope to distract her by doing so? 'I seem to recall Katherine enjoyed herself for weeks at his expense before Petruchio tamed her.'

They reached the library and he'd yet to make a suitable rejoinder. A lone footman was waiting for them and flung open the doors and bowed them inside. 'How the devil did he get here?' The duke wasn't impressed. He waved the man away with an angry gesture.

Rosamond walked across the book-lined room and curled up on a wide, well padded armchair. Why was he so cross? Did she dare ask him, or would he then turn his irritation upon her? 'Your grace, someone overheard us say we were heading for the library and sent the servant ahead. Perhaps you're

120

not aware that at Hathersage Hall the walls do literally have ears.'

He shook his head and with a resigned sigh collapsed on a similar chair positioned opposite her. 'Now what nonsense are you babbling, child? Explain.'

'There are narrow passageways running through this house. My grandfather wished his staff to be invisible, to be able to move unseen from chamber to chamber. All the major rooms have a servants' door hidden in the wall somewhere.'

'Well I'll be damned! I've never heard such nonsense. I've a good mind to remove myself to the Dower House when it's ready and leave your mother and sisters here.'

Her gasp stopped him in mid-tirade. She wasn't sure if she was more shocked by his language or his comment. 'You are going to banish my family from here? I — '

He smiled, quite unrepentant. 'No, you ninnyhammer, just your mother.

I've no objection to your siblings remaining with us, which leads nicely to the reason we are here.' He sat forward and fixed her with an unnerving stare. 'I have decided we shall be married with due state, not in a rushed ceremony. Would you like to have a ball after the wedding breakfast? Presumably there are neighbours and so on you would like to invite. I thought to postpone the wedding for three weeks. Will that be sufficient time for arrangements to be put in hand?'

'A proper wedding? In a church with flowers and guests? A wedding breakfast and a ball?' She was speechless. The very idea appalled her. She could only bear it if the deed was done in private. To be paraded down the aisle as if she were a willing participant was the outside of enough.

He was smiling, waiting for her leap to her feet and exclaim with joy. She drew breath to tell him exactly what she thought of his ridiculous suggestion, but then hesitated. Had he not just removed her from the study, sensing somehow she was reluctant to enter? He was offering her a wedding that would be Millie's dream. How could she tell him that an elaborate occasion was her nightmare?

'Actually, I would much prefer to be married immediately with only my sisters and mother present. I do thank you for your kind thoughts, sir, but I would prefer something simple. What you had in mind previously will suit me perfectly.'

'Are you quite sure you don't wish a fuss to be made? I intended to give you time to become accustomed to the notion of becoming my duchess.'

'I fear I might not be able to go through with the marriage if you allow me so much time to think.' This wasn't exactly what she intended to say, but she couldn't pretend to be pleased when she was the reverse. If the union was to work then they must be honest with each other, however painful that might be at the time.

His expression changed from friendly to formal. 'In which case, make sure that you're in the drawing room at ten o'clock tomorrow morning. I shall inform the duchess, and no doubt you will do the same for your sisters.' He stood up, and behind his glacial facade there was regret in his eyes. She couldn't let him depart without explaining the reason for the cruel rejection of his kindness.

'Please, don't go. Let me explain.' He was on his feet and without thinking, she moved towards him, holding out her hands in supplication. He ignored them and remained stationary, but at least he didn't back away.

'Well? I'm waiting.'

'I'm not a child, sir, but a woman grown, and know when I say my vows tomorrow they are unbreakable. We will be committed to each other for better or worse for the rest of our lives. If this arrangement is to work, then I sincerely believe we must be totally honest with each other. I would never lie to you, and pray that you never do so either.' He was listening now and his eyes were watchful, rather than accusatory. 'I have told you my views on matrimony — that I've no interest in domestic matters and even less in producing children. However, I'm well aware I must change. You told me yesterday I have six months to become accustomed to being your duchess before I become your wife, and I'm profoundly grateful for that respite. I pray that in the interim we can develop a genuine affection for each other which will make what follows so much easier for both of us. I realise children are inevitable, but I hope you'll not require me to produce one every year.'

She hadn't realised he had closed the gap whilst she'd been talking and was now a few scant inches from her. 'I applaud your honesty, sweetheart, and give you my word that I'll always speak the truth, however difficult it might be.' He took her hands and clasped them lightly. 'For the first time since this debacle began I am hopeful there might be a happy ending.'

'This union has been forced upon both of us by circumstances beyond our control — it's an arranged marriage with no love on either side. But as you say, sir, we must hope we'll one day find pleasure in each other's company and learn to hold each other in affection.' How formal she sounded — more like her mother than herself. Should she lighten the mood with a jest of some sort?

'I dislike being addressed as 'your grace' and 'sir' — I can do nothing about the former, but from this point on I insist that you call me by my given name.' His mouth curved a little. 'No one uses that; it will be pleasant to hear my name. It's Elliott, by the by.'

'Mama will be scandalised by such informality, but Elliott and Rosamond it shall be from now on. My parents referred to each other as 'Duke' and 'Duchess' throughout their married life.' She placed a hand on his arm.

'Now everything's agreed between us, I think we must see Mama.' She smiled at him. 'I do hope you aren't serious with your suggestion that we live in the Dower House and leave Hathersage to her?'

'I suppose we must remain here and banish your mother. Will your sisters wish to remain with us or accompany the dowager?'

'Remain here, no question about that. Why would they wish to give up their luxurious apartments and move elsewhere if they didn't have to?' A lurking footman snatched open the doors as they reached them and Elliott scowled.

'I'm not comfortable with servants creeping about the place and eaves-dropping on matters that are of no concern to them.'

'You must ignore them. It's how things are in an establishment of this size. They are all loyal to this family and would never, ever gossip about anything they became privy to by accident. We have around fifty indoor staff and the same outside. The village of Hathersage depends for its existence entirely on this place, as do dozens of labourers and tenant farmers. We have a duty — '

'Thank you, Rosamond, but I don't require a lecture from you. It is duty that finds me here, forced to marry a reluctant bride, when I would much prefer to be living a simple life elsewhere and be free to do as I please with whom I please.'

At his heartfelt words her childish fantasies, that he might actually wish to marry her despite the circumstances, vanished. He'd been hiding his true feelings well, far better than she had. In some ways this made things easier. They were both making the ultimate sacrifice — giving up their lives in the name of duty. An unwanted bubble of mirth escaped with a hiss and he looked down at her.

'Something amuses you, my dear? Will you share it with me?'

They were approaching the grand

hall and there would be no time for levity once they entered the drawing-room. 'I find I'm becoming alarmingly like my mother. Even my private thoughts are being invaded by her formality.'

'I'm relieved to hear it's only your thoughts that are changing. God forbid someone as beautiful as you should turn into — '

'Elliott, you mustn't say such things even in jest. Mama was not always so strict and cold. Unhappy circumstances have changed her into what she is today. Beneath her hideous turbans she still has beautiful golden hair.'

He raised an eyebrow and she couldn't help responding with a smile. Walking beside him gave her much-needed confidence. Mama could no longer treat her as an unwanted embarrassment; she was certain he would never allow his future wife to be treated disrespectfully, even by a parent.

Her mother was seated on an

uncomfortable upright chair and was glaring down the room as if daring either Elliott or herself to speak before being spoken to. Her sisters were sitting on a day bed on the far side of the room — indeed, they couldn't be further from Mama if they tried.

'Have courage, little one. We shall rout the dragon between us.' His words were whispered into her ear and she squeezed his arm to show she understood.

They marched, step perfect, down the drawing-room. Never had this chamber seemed so large, or the distance from the double doors so great. Without his support she doubted she would have accomplished the walk without stumbling over her feet.

He halted a few feet from her mother but didn't bow, but merely inclined his head a fraction. She would take her cue from him and not venture a remark until asked to. 'Duchess, Rosamond and I are in accord. We shall be married in this room at ten o'clock tomorrow morning. The rector has been informed.'

A strained silence stretched between them and she wanted to say something to break the tension, but a slight shake of the head indicated he wished her to remain quiet. Why didn't Mama say something? How long was this to last? Then Millie squealed, making everyone jump. For an awful moment Rosamond thought her sister was going to make an embarrassing scene.

'Dearest Rosamond, thank you for taking this unpleasant duty from my shoulders. Handsome though he is, your duke would not do for me. I am relying on you to give me a splendid season and find me a more amenable duke of my own.'

Hardly the most tactful of responses, but her sister was famous for her beauty not her wit. 'Thank you, Millie. I'm glad you're happy for me.' Elliott was gently vibrating beside her. She risked a glance and saw he was biting his lip in a vain attempt to hold back his laughter.

'Flora, Elizabeth, are you not to wish me well?'

The girls threw a nervous look at their mama and then decided to change allegiance. All three girls jumped from the chaise longue and ran towards Rosamond, chattering and laughing. She put her arms around her younger sisters and drew all three girls to the far end of the room in order to leave the battlefield clear for her future husband.

★　★　★

Elliott watched his future bride gather her sisters around her like a mother hen and escort them out of danger. There was something about Rosamond that moved him — she had an indefinable quality that he'd never met in a woman before. His former liaisons had been with willing women of the *demimonde* and he had no experience at all of gently bred young ladies. The girl he was to marry tomorrow morning was certainly not demure, and had a forthrightness about her that appealed to him.

He turned his attention to the unpleasant woman still silent before him. Best get this out of the way so he could concentrate on what was important. 'It is a matter of supreme indifference to me, madam, whether you approve or disapprove of my actions. However, if you wish to remain part of your daughters' lives, I suggest you at least pretend to be pleased.'

Still no reaction. He closed the distance between them and spoke softly so only the duchess could hear. 'Your daughters will remain with me and my wife when you remove yourself to the Dower House next week. Rosamond shall arrange to bring them out and unless you make an effort to be civil, you will be excluded from every family event. I shall provide you with sufficient funds to live well, but you will remain in seclusion unless I give you leave to join us.'

Her complexion paled and her fan

snapped between her fingers. 'I do not like you, sir. I doubt that I ever will. However, because my darling son is dead, you are indisputably the head of the household and the eighth Duke of Hathersage. I have no intention of mouldering away in seclusion, and you do not hold my purse strings.' Her voice rang out and every syllable was clearly heard by her children.

This was news to him, but then he'd scarcely had time to go through the mountain of papers the family lawyers had presented him with. 'In which case, Duchess, might I wish you *bon voyage* and hope that your journey might be long and permanent.'

She scrambled to her feet, scattering the debris from her broken fan about her feet. 'I have a delightful house in Brook Street and a substantial estate in Hertfordshire. My father was an earl and I a lady in my own right.' Beads of spittle collected on her mouth and he took an involuntary step backwards. 'I give you fair warning, sir. You have made a grievous error today. I am considered a good friend but make an even better enemy. For all your wealth, you are no gentleman and I shall make it my life's work to ensure you get no pleasure from usurping my beloved son.' She stalked the length of the room, looking neither right nor left, and her daughters watched her leave in open-mouthed astonishment.

Buggeration! What was wrong with him? For years he'd commanded his regiment without alienating his officers or his men, and yet today he'd allowed his personal feelings to colour his judgement. However unpleasant the dowager was, she would be his mother-in-law very shortly, and grand-mother to any children he and Rosamond might have in the future. His mishandling of the situation was likely to have unpleasant ramifications for years to come if he didn't somehow sweet-talk the duchess into an accep-tance of his position. Rosamond was attempting to repair the damage by telling her sisters what a wonderful time they would have in London next season when they were presented. Dealing with a parcel of women was worse than facing a cavalry charge from Napoleon's finest troops. He was out of his depth and needed the help of his friend to extricate him from the pit he'd dug for himself and his future wife.

He didn't care what society thought of him, but he now had the responsibility of finding husbands for Rosamond's sisters, and they needed to have an unblemished reputation in order to find themselves partners of equal rank.

He strolled across to join the young ladies, and the golden girls immediately were quiet and watched him warily. Only Rosamond was pleased to see him. 'I must apologise — ' he began.

'Pray do not, sir. Mama has a fearful temper and says the most dreadful things, but always comes round in the end and usually regrets her unkindness. We are used to her outbursts, are we not, girls?'

Millie looked unconvinced. 'She's never said such dreadful things to anyone apart from you and Papa, and I don't remember her ever apologising. Do you, Flora, or you, Elizabeth?'

'Lady Amelia, please allow me to borrow your sister. We have things we need to discuss for tomorrow. I thought we could all spend a few weeks in Bath once matters are settled here. I'm sure that you will all need to replenish your wardrobes. Perhaps you would like to send for the London seamstress to bring samples and fashion plates immediately?'

This was the perfect antidote to the previous unpleasantness, and Rosamond smiled with such sweetness that his heart all but skipped a beat. 'Bath? I've heard such wonderful reports of the balls and parties held there. Are you quite sure you wish us to order new gowns, sir?'

He smiled at her innocent enthusiasm. 'As many as you like, my dear. We

137

shall consider it a practice for the real thing next year.' He frowned. He was promising them a summer of fun and had no idea how to go about arranging it. 'I shall leave you young ladies to discuss what feminine fripperies you require. Pray excuse me; I have urgent business to attend to.'

Rosamond caught his eye and winked at him in a most unladylike way. His spirits lifted. With a girl like her at his side, anything was possible. But first he must find Davenport and enlist his help to organise the visit to this fashionable town. He had a sinking feeling he might have promised a treat he couldn't provide. Obtaining a suitably luxurious house for the remainder of the summer season might well prove impossible so late in the year.

8

'Will the duke really take us all to Bath, Rosamond?' Millie asked anxiously as soon as Elliott was gone.

'Of course he will. He's a man of his word. Do you have a recent copy of *Ackerman's Repository*, Millie? Bring it to my apartment and we'll peruse it together. I do believe I'll send a messenger to Madame Ducray and ask her to come here by post.' She hesitated, not sure exactly how to proceed. Until tomorrow morning Mama was officially the lady of the house, but after her unpleasant tirade she was fairly sure her mother had abdicated all responsibility for her daughters and the household.

'Gibson will arrange it for you, Rosamond. I'm sure he understands how things are, and that you are the new mistress of Hathersage,' Millie said helpfully.

Flora rushed to the bell strap and pulled it vigorously. 'Everyone will have heard about what happened here — Mama made sure of that.' She shook her head and her ringlets danced. 'Anyway, you are much nicer than Mama, and even the duke is not as awful as we first thought. I think he looks quite nice when he smiles, don't you, Elizabeth?'

Things were moving too fast for Rosamond. The arrival of the duke had turned their lives upside-down and caused a rift between Mama and the rest of them that might never heal. Papa had warned her that things would be difficult after his death, but could have had no notion Millie wouldn't be the new duchess or that Elliott would permanently alienate his widow.

'I'm sure he'll be delighted to hear your views, Flora. Do you wish me to convey them to him?' The look of absolute horror on her sister's face made them all laugh, which was what Rosamond had intended.

The door opened and Gibson stepped through, his face grave. 'You rang, my lady?'

Rosamond explained and he almost smiled. 'Might I be permitted to say, my lady, that I think a visit to Bath is an excellent idea. Do you wish me to send Mrs Turner to see you?'

'Thank you, Gibson, but I don't think that will be necessary. Kindly tell Turner to prepare the household for the move. We will depart as soon as the duke has made the necessary arrangements, but I'm not sure exactly when that will be.' She was ducking out of the meeting with the housekeeper, as Turner had been appointed by Mama and was likely to refuse to take orders from anyone but her mother until Rosamond was actually the new duchess.

Planning the move of such an enormous household without the expert guidance of the housekeeper was going to be an arduous task. Was this what Mama meant when she said she was going to make life difficult for them? For a moment Rosamond quailed at the prospect, but then pushed such feeble-minded thoughts aside. Once she was married she would be able to hire and dismiss any member of the indoor staff. She would make it abundantly clear to anyone who created problems that she would get rid of them without hesitation and appoint more amenable servants.

* * *

Elliott found his friend hiding in the library. 'Coward. I could have done with your support when braving the dowager duchess.'

'God help you, Bromley — you certainly stuck your finger in the hornets' nest this time. I doubt you'll turn her up sweet without a miracle.'

'As always your encouragement is invaluable to me, Davenport. Jesting aside, I promised to take the household to Bath for the remainder of the summer. Have I a hope in hell of finding anywhere suitable to live?' He eyed the decanter of brandy kept on the sideboard and was sorely tempted to pour himself a stiff drink, but thought better of it. He needed a clear head, and drowning his sorrows would help no one. Instead he joined his companion on the enormous Chesterfield. 'Well, Davenport, can you step into the breach for me?'

'As it happens, I can do better than that. A great aunt left me a substantial property in that very place, and although I intended to rent it out for the season, I never got round to it. It's fully staffed so you won't need to take any servants, apart from personal attendants.'

'I've never set foot in the place, but I gather Bath is a desirable watering hole for fortune-hunters and the elderly. I can't imagine why my new family wish to go there. Where exactly is your house?'

'I misremember the exact address,

but I visited the old biddy occasionally when on leave and it's in the most fashionable area — a short walk from the circulating library, assembly rooms, bathing rooms and beach.'

'Good grief! I never thought to hear you speak of all those things in one sentence. Send one of my staff with instructions to ready the house. I will, of course, pay you whatever is appropriate for the lease.'

'You'll do no such thing, my friend. Consider the use of my house a wedding gift. I hope I can accompany you on this excursion? You're going to need my vigilance to keep the undesirable young men away from your beautiful wards.'

'The more I consider this, the less I like the sound of it.' He stretched his arms and yawned. 'Domesticity is more tiring than fighting the French. Without your support I might take the coward's way and abandon my unwanted responsibilities.'

'How can you be unhappy about

being given the title of Duke of Hathersage and untold riches to go with it? Good God, Bromley, you've also been given a beautiful bride — I can't believe any other man in Christendom would call this bad luck.'

'I wasn't born to rule. As you know, my father was a country squire and my mother the daughter of a vicar. I am certain he didn't know he was in direct line to this title. The connection is so remote I'm surprised they found me at all. After a lifetime of soldiering all I wanted was to become a country squire on a small estate and involve myself in farming.'

His friend looked unconvinced. 'First I've heard of it, old fellow, you would die of boredom within a year without any challenges. Running this huge establishment and marrying Lady Rosamond should keep you interested for the remainder of your days.' He laughed and punched Elliott on the shoulder. 'I'm hoping I might take Lady Amelia off your hands. I'm halfway to being head-over-heels in love with her already. Do I have your permission to woo her?'

'I can't think of anyone I'd like better as a brother. Although I give you fair warning, the girl is determined to find herself a duke — not sure a peer of the realm is grand enough for her. I've never enquired — are you in a position to support my ward in the way she is accustomed to?'

'It's strange that we've been friends for so long and yet know so little about each other. I'm the son of the Earl of Silchester and will inherit that title when my parent kicks the bucket. As he's in his prime, I pray that won't be for some considerable time. I've an ample trust fund and a decent country house in Essex.' He rubbed his eyes before continuing. 'Like you, I never expected to be the heir. Pa would never have bought me my colours but for my oldest brother Simon being in rude health and an ideal custodian for the family wealth.'

'I take it he died in some accident or

other? Was this recent? I'm surprised you didn't resign your commission immediately.'

'He died a year after he contracted the sweating sickness — if you recall I was rather low just before Waterloo. I couldn't return for the funeral, and as the war was won there was no necessity for me to resign.'

'Why didn't you tell me? Are not friends supposed to help each other through difficult times? Dammit, I've been complaining whilst you've been suffering a grievous loss. Shouldn't you be at home comforting your parents?'

'I returned briefly, but my presence wasn't welcome. Neither of them have accepted Simon's loss, and therefore seeing me just rubbed salt in the wound. My mother is draped in black and weeps a lot — more than a fellow can stand.'

Elliott had been doing arithmetic in his head. 'It must be a year since your brother died, so you're free to gad about society without offending. I sincerely wish you'd shared your loss with me, but I'm relieved you've fully recovered and are ready to set up your own establishment. This makes you more eligible as a partner for Amelia; I'll make sure Rosamond drops it into a conversation before we leave.' He stood up. 'If the girl doesn't want you, that's her decision. I want all three to be able to choose for themselves. Marrying from necessity isn't the ideal way to begin one's married life, and I've no wish for Rosamond's sisters to suffer as she has.'

'I'll squire the young ladies around Bath, thus leaving you and your new wife to become better acquainted. Do you intend to abandon your mother-in-law when you go?'

'On that subject, Davenport, I was hoping you could give me some advice. I mishandled the situation and pushed the dowager into a corner. Small wonder that she savaged me.'

'I think you would be wise to let

things settle before attempting a reconciliation. Let the air clear whilst you're residing in Bath, and possibly she'll be feeling more amenable when you return. Mind you, from what she shouted, I gather she intends to move to properties of her own. Have you checked with your lawyers that she does indeed have free title to the London house and estate she mentioned?'

'Dawkins should be here this afternoon and I'll discuss the matter with him then. Shall we wear our regimentals for tomorrow's ceremony?'

'Absolutely. All that scarlet and gold frogging cannot fail to impress the ladies. If the duchess is not to attend, who will be your other witness?'

'The lawyer is staying here until after the ceremony in order to release the funds immediately it's completed. He must stand in if necessary.'

He was heartily sick of everything to do with Hathersage and its problems — no, that wasn't quite correct. If he hadn't inherited the title he wouldn't have met Rosamond, and marrying her would more than recompense for all the rest. If the dratted lawyer didn't appear in the next quarter of an hour he would get out of the house. Although he'd ridden once this morning, the estate manager was eager to give him a conducted tour of the nearest farms within his demesne.

★ ★ ★

Madame Ducray arrived post-haste with two assistants carrying fashion plates and swatches of material, plus a milliner. Rosamond's sisters were exclaiming in ecstasy and ready to order far too many expensive gowns. She'd submitted to the tedious business of being measured and then asked Millie to choose for her, but follow certain rules.

'I don't like fussy gowns with frills and furbelows, nor do I want to emphasise my lack of bosom. Green is my favourite colour and I detest pink.

Apart from that I'll rely on your good taste.'

She had already informed the seamstress that no expense was to be spared and the new wardrobes for each of them were to be paraded in Bath. 'We intend to depart at the end of next week, madame, and would like as many of the items here before then. The rest must be sent on as soon as possible.'

'Will you not stay, Rosamond?' Millie asked her. 'I've never seen so many pretty patterns as this. Even Papa at his most generous never allowed us to purchase so much. Are you absolutely certain the duke won't be angry at our extravagance?'

'He's a man of his word, as I've already told you before; he wishes you to be happy, and to make up for the lack of funds this past twelve months he is happy to indulge you now. I trust you not to overspend, Millie. If you do so, you might not find your guardian is as generous next year.'

Her sister nodded. 'I understand,

Rosamond. I'll ensure the girls are sensible.'

Rosamond craved fresh air and on impulse returned to her apartment to change into a promenade gown. She arrived to find it in disarray. 'Jane, whatever's going on? I wish to walk — will you find something suitable in this chaos?'

'My lady, instructions have come from his grace to move you to the . . . your . . . the apartment next to his.'

'Does my mother know of this?'

'Yes, my lady. She's already packing to leave. Her abigail says they are to live in Hertfordshire somewhere and not in the Dower House.'

'I feared she would storm off in high dudgeon after this morning. Don't move anything until you're certain her apartment is empty. Now, a gown, bonnet, and walking boots, please.'

In less than fifteen minutes she was on her way down, having assured her maid she had no need of an escort. Her bonnet was swinging from one hand;

she had no intention of putting it on until she absolutely had to. This afternoon she would exit through the front door and keep the footmen on their toes. She was crossing the vast expanse of black and white tiles when she was hailed from the gallery.

'Are you going out, my dear?'

She spun, sending the skirt of her pale green muslin swirling around her ankles. 'How observant you are, sir. And might I hazard a guess that you intend to ride?' He was leaning on the balustrade in his riding coat.

He laughed and the rich, warm sound echoed around the empty space. 'I was intending to ride around the estate but will take a carriage instead. Will you accompany me?'

She didn't hesitate. A drive with her future husband was exactly what she wanted. 'Yes, I'd love to. I can direct you to the village and the nearest farms.'

'Excellent — I'll send word to the stables to bring out the barouche.' He grinned. 'I gather the travelling carriage isn't available today. I suppose you're aware your redoubtable parent is departing this very afternoon?'

'I am indeed. Shall we stroll around the gardens until the carriage is brought round?'

He had bounded down the stairs and was now at her side. 'Devil take it! I believe that damned lawyer has finally arrived. I'm sorry, sweetheart, but I must cancel my offer. Duty calls.' He turned to greet the middle-aged gentleman in a dusty, old-fashioned frockcoat who was being bowed into the hall. 'By the way, you look remarkably smart in that ensemble. No doubt the matching bonnet will be put on eventually.'

Smiling at his banter, she nodded politely to the visitor and continued to the gardens, only remembering to pull on the hated headgear at the last minute. Although Capability Brown had redesigned the park, Mama had insisted on keeping the maze and the rose gardens. She headed in that direction, as the roses were at their very best just now.

She was greeted by the head gardener. 'Have you come to choose the blooms for your bouquet, my lady? My lads have instructions to pick sufficient flowers to decorate inside as well. Do you have any roses in mind?'

Until that moment she'd not considered flowers of any sort for the ceremony tomorrow. She hadn't even decided on her outfit, thinking that of little importance — after all, they were marrying through expediency, not because they wished to be with each other. 'I think white, cream and gold would be perfect, if possible. I'd like some greenery too.'

'I'll make you a lovely posy, my lady. I know you like things simple. What about a matching wreath of rosebuds for your hair?'

'That would be delightful. Please have them upstairs by nine o'clock tomorrow morning.'

Her pleasure in the excursion had gone with all this talk of weddings. No doubt there were dozens of vital things to organise, and she really couldn't spend any longer wandering around the garden. She blinked back tears. Mama should have been attending to these details. If her favourite daughter Millie had been the bride, no doubt her mother would have been fully involved. By leaving so conspicuously the day before the ceremony, she was making it abundantly clear to the neighbourhood and the *ton* that she disapproved of the union.

Before Charles had died, Mama had been one of the leading hostesses in society. Her soirees and routs, musicales and supper parties had been the talk of the town. Her success was legendary among the cognoscenti and it was perfectly possible that, if she desired, she could blacken Elliott's name so that none of them would be received in society despite his title and fabulous wealth.

With this lowering thought upper-most in her mind, she returned to her apartment determined to enjoy the remainder of the afternoon with her beloved sisters.

Jane was wringing her hands when Rosamond reached her apartment. 'My lady, I'm at a loss to know what to do. His grace was most insistent you should be in your new apartment this evening, but the duchess has changed her mind and is refusing to budge.'

'That's a good thing, not something to complain about. I'll speak to the duke immediately and explain the situation, and then return to select my ensemble for tomorrow.'

Her sisters were still engrossed in fashion plates and silks and satins. Madame the milliner and her assistants were busy scribbling their requests. She had to raise her voice to attract Millie's attention. 'Millie dearest, if you can bear to leave your list of requests for a short while, I'd like your help to decide what to wear for my wedding. I'm having cream, white and gold roses for my bouquet, and my gown must complement those.'

'We would love to, wouldn't we?' Millie clapped her hands and Flora and Elizabeth ran over. 'Surely you're going to stay this time, Rosamond?'

'I'll be back shortly; if you could lay out the garments you think will do I'll make my decision when I return.'

She was about to barge into the study where Elliott was having his meeting with the lawyer, when she thought better of it and knocked politely instead. Receiving no response, she knocked louder, and this time she was told to be about her business in no uncertain terms by the man she was about to marry.

How dare he shout at her as if she were a servant? She flung the door open and stormed in. 'I don't care if you are the King of Sheba. I won't be spoken to so rudely in my own house.'

Elliott was on his feet and shook his head as if confused by her comment. 'What the devil are you talking about?

Why are you here?' Then he understood and he smiled, quite disarming her. 'And, in case you'd forgotten, my love, I am the Duke of Hathersage and not the King of Sheba.'

The lawyer listened open-mouthed to this exchange. He was also on his feet and nodding and bowing in turn. 'My lady, your grace, shall I absent myself?'

Elliott waved him back to his seat and beckoned her to join him. He moved a third chair next to his and waited until she was seated. 'Tell me, what burr has stuck under your saddle this time?'

'Mama is no longer leaving today, therefore I cannot move into the apartment. I believe she might have reconsidered and is now reconciled to our marriage.'

'Unfortunately, you couldn't be more wrong. Things are even more serious than before. I was about to send for you and explain what Dawkins has told me. As this information has been relayed to the duchess it might well explain her decision.'

9

'Tell me at once, Elliott. I can't believe matters could be any worse.'

'Dawkins, it might be best if you told Lady Rosamond what we've just discovered.'

The lawyer cleared his throat and shuffled some papers nervously. 'The duchess was under the misapprehension that the estate in Surrey and a townhouse in Brook Street were hers. In fact they pass to the next duchess on her wedding, which is you, my lady. Also, the generous annuity will cease; from tomorrow this also becomes yours, and therefore your parent will be entirely dependent on the duke.'

She looked from one to the other in puzzlement. 'Why is that a bad thing? If I temporarily hold the title to these properties, then I can give her permission to move there. As for her annuity, can you not reinstate it?'

'Believe me, I've already suggested this,' said Elliott, 'but she threw the offer back in my face. She said in no uncertain terms that she intends to remain where she is unless I'm prepared to have her physically removed. I won't repeat the uncomplimentary thing she said about us, as you're sufficiently distressed already.'

'Why should she wish to remain somewhere she's unhappy?' Then she recalled something that had been mentioned in conversation before Elliott had arrived. 'I know what has upset her. We all believed you would wish to marry Millie and if that had been the case, Mama had every intention of remaining in charge. Millie would have agreed to hand over the reins of the establishment whether she wished to or not.'

Elliott crashed his fist down on the desk, scattering papers in all directions. 'So as she cannot have her way, she'll do her best to make our lives intolerable. Over my dead body,

Rosamond. She has issued a challenge and I intend to take her up on that.' He was on his feet and striding towards the door before she could restrain him. He was in the corridor when she caught up with him.

'Please, you cannot speak to her when you are enraged. Whatever she says or does, she is my mama, and I love her.' Her words had the desired effect and he halted. She was about to repeat her plea when he spoke softly so only she could hear.

'Sweetheart, we can't let her stay in your apartment. Tomorrow morning it will be yours by right.'

'Then please leave it until after we're married, and then she will be in the wrong and the staff will know it. Even those closest to her might then lose sympathy with her.'

He remained unconvinced and she placed both hands on his arm. 'Is there anything I can do to persuade you from your course?'

His eyes glinted and his mouth

curved in a wicked smile. 'If you agree to move into my apartment then the problem will be solved.'

A wave of something that could have been excitement flooded her already overheated body. He was suggesting she become his true wife immediately. To save her mother from further upset she would do anything, even this. 'I will do as you ask, but it's under duress and isn't what we agreed previously.'

His free hand came up to stroke her face with a gentleness she'd not expected. 'I'm a brute to tease you. Stay where you are, little one, and the duchess shall remain where she is, at least until tomorrow.'

Her fingers unclenched from his arm and she stepped away stiffly. 'I don't appreciate your levity, sir, on such an intimate subject. The more I get to know you, the less I like you. Mama was right to label you a rough soldier and unfitted for the position thrust upon you.' She hadn't intended to say anything so harsh, but the relief at being reprieved from sharing his bed had loosened her tongue disastrously.

He raked her with an icy glance. 'And you, Lady Rosamond, might not look like your mother, but you are similar in every other way — you are both viper-tongued shrews.' He turned his back and returned to his interrupted meeting, slamming the door behind him.

They had been slowly establishing a rapport and now she had ruined it for both of them. He had called her a shrew and she had labelled him as uncouth and stupid. There was still the matter of dinner to get through tonight and she could hardly refuse to go down a second time. She shuddered. Would Mama appear or remain in her rooms?

She took her time returning to her apartment so that she was fully composed and able to hide her distress from her sisters. Madame was delighted to see her.

'We have everything we need and are departing immediately. I'll have every seamstress working on your new gowns as soon as I get back. I guarantee there will be several gowns completed and ready for you to take on your *vacance*. I thank you, my lady, for the order, and I promise you will not be disappointed.' Her minions had gathered up the scattered samples of material, had all their notes carefully packed away, and were ready to leave.

'I appreciate your prompt arrival and look forward to seeing the results of your endeavours in due course.' Millie had already sent for a footman to escort the party out, and a carriage was waiting to transport them to the coaching inn where they would return by post. To travel this way was exorbitantly expensive, but today Rosamond didn't care about the extravagance. She had far weightier matters on her mind.

When they were in private, she gathered her sisters around her and explained what had happened. 'So you see, it's possible our mother might be reconsidering her hasty words. She and the duke will never be friends, but I shall be satisfied if they can remain in the same room without being at daggers drawn.'

'Don't you mind having to stay here at the back of the house when you should be in the best apartment next to him?' Flora asked.

'I love my rooms, Flora, and the longer I can remain here the happier I'll be. I scarcely know my future husband and it will be easier becoming friends if we're not forever falling over each other upstairs.' This was fustian, but they happily accepted her prevarication.

'Now show me, what you have chosen for tomorrow?'

Millie pointed to the four gowns draped over the backs of various chairs. 'We think these are the best match for the flowers you've selected, Rosamond. I'd no idea you had so many pretty dresses; I swear you've not worn any of these.'

'I've no interest in such things, as you know.' She examined each in turn and was forced to admit that they were all excellent choices. 'I think this gossamer-fine muslin, with a green petticoat and cream overskirt, will do perfectly. The exquisite golden rosebuds attached to the neckline and cuffs complement the outfit. Good heavens, you've found matching stockings and slippers. Thank goodness there's no necessity for me to wear a bonnet indoors, for I'm certainly not putting on one of those monstrosities you've found.' Laughing at their shocked expressions, she picked up the nearest, the brim of which was so deep she could scarcely see where she was going. 'I feel as if I'm wearing blinkers. This hat is certainly not one I chose. I believe Mama must have been instrumental in its arrival here.'

'It's the height of fashion, Rosamond, and if you really don't want it, then may I have it please?' Flora smiled hopefully and she tossed it over.

'As it's considered bad luck for a bride to meet her future husband the night before the wedding, I've decided we shall have an alfresco meal in the summerhouse. This will mean the duke and his friend may dine without fear of meeting me. We don't need to change; we can play shuttlecock and walk in the maze as we used to when we were young.'

The suggestion was received with enthusiasm, and one of the willing chambermaids hurried downstairs with instructions. She assumed her mother would wish to remain in her chamber, so arranged for a tray to be sent there. The remainder of the afternoon slipped by pleasantly enough and she was able to almost forget what was going to happen at ten o'clock the next morning.

When Flora saw the food being carried out for their picnic supper, Rosamond was as eager as her siblings to run into the garden. This would be the last time they would be together in this way because, however much she disliked the idea, when she was mistress of Hathersage everything would change.

★　★　★

'Come away from the window, Bromley. You know it's bad luck for you to see your bride this evening,' Davenport said.

'Things could not be worse than they already are, I'm marrying a girl who hates me and I can see no happy outcome for either of us.' His friend wandered across the drawing room to join him. 'See how happy she is with her sisters. She's scarcely out of the schoolroom and is being forced into marriage with a man who will make her a wretched husband.'

'I thought you were eager to marry Lady Rosamond — that from the moment you saw her yesterday you knew she was your perfect match.'

'I am, and she is — I would be the happiest man in the kingdom to be marrying such a lovely young woman, if she only shared my feelings. Things might have been so different without the interference of her dreadful mother.'

Reluctantly, he moved from the open French windows, not wishing to be seen by the quartet of happy girls playing in the waist-high maze. 'I'm closing Hathersage whilst we're away — did I tell you? I'm having the whole place cleaned and our apartments redecorated and refurnished. Both are old-fashioned and I'm sure Rosamond and I will be happier with more modern furniture and decoration.'

'And what will happen to the present occupant of the duchess's apartment?'

'She will move to the Dower House, taking her coterie of servants with her. Gibson has matters in hand and knows exactly who needs to be weeded out before Rosamond takes control of the household. Good God, man, there are more than six bedchambers and a plethora of reception rooms and servants' quarters in that house. She will be living in the lap of luxury at my expense in a house that would suit me far better than this.'

'I think you've rather missed the point, old fellow. How do you think Lady Rosamond would feel if she were to be evicted penniless by her daughter-in-law after having been mistress of Hathersage?'

Elliott was so shocked by this comment that he stepped back incautiously and tumbled over the arm of a loveseat, throwing his glass of cognac in his face, much to the amusement of his friend. His language turned the air blue as he hurtled upright and Davenport recoiled at his expression. 'How could I have failed to grasp this basic fact? God in his heaven! In the past two days I've blundered from one catastrophic decision to another. What in the hell is wrong with me?' This being a rhetorical question, his friend had the common sense not to answer. 'As far as I know I've never made a poor decision in the field — no man under my command has lost his life through my stupidity.' He wiped the brandy from his face and strode over to pour himself a refill. 'Can I somehow retrieve the situation? I fear that not only the battle but the entire war might already be lost.'

'Don't lose heart. These are the preliminary skirmishes. We can discuss your strategy and still come out the victors.'

'To be honest, I don't give a damn about the dowager. My only concern is to mend my fences with Rosamond. She's giving up so much more than me. I've sown my wild oats and I'm ready to settle down. She hasn't even had a season in town. She's barely twenty years of age and from tomorrow will have this monstrosity draped around her neck for the rest of her life.'

'Until you kick the bucket, my friend, and then no doubt she'll be evicted like her mother.' Elliott aimed a none-too-gentle punch at his friend's shoulder and Davenport staggered back. 'I apologise — a jest in poor taste. Lady

Rosamond is nothing like her mother; she's kind and loving. Your son will be begging her to remain within the family.'

'That's true, but if we have no boys to inherit, things will be quite different.' His eyes darkened at the thought of what must come first if there were to be children from the union. One thing was in no doubt: Rosamond made him feel like a young man again. She was the most desirable woman he'd ever encountered. Staying out of her bed for the agreed six months was going to be the most difficult thing he'd ever had to do.

★ ★ ★

Rosamond slept little and was up at first light. Jane had left out her habit, but this morning she intended to wear only her breeches and not the heavy skirt. She rummaged on the shelves of her closet and found the items she was looking for. She had hidden some

173

garments there which had belonged to her brother for no other reason than she couldn't bear to lose him entirely. She'd never intended to wear the items, but her brother had been a similar size to her — a little broader in the shoulders perhaps — but she was hopeful his riding coat, waistcoat, shirt and cravat would fit her.

The shirt was a little long in the sleeve and the waistcoat rather loose, but this was perfect as it disguised what feminine curves she had. The jacket was a deep moss green with black collar and lapels — her favourite colour, which was why she'd stolen this one. The skirt of the jacket fell to her knees, thus amply covering her rear end. With the neck cloth suitably arranged, all she had to do was make her escape without being seen.

At this hour not even the servants were about and she was obliged to unbolt the side door herself. A clock somewhere in the house struck five — she was an hour earlier than expected. She might have to tack up the duke's horse herself. The stable yard was never silent; there was always the sound of horses shifting in their boxes. To her surprise, Albert was waiting for her.

'Good morning, my lady. I'll saddle the gelding for you right away.'

She stepped up onto the mounting block, her heart hammering as she constantly glanced over her shoulder in case the duke arrived unexpectedly. She could no longer think of him by his given name after his cruel words last night. But when the spirited horse was led out, she began to regret her decision. Why did she wish to risk a nasty fall and further antagonise the owner?

Then she forgot her fears and was lost in admiration for the horse that had travelled the continent with the duke and brought him safely home again. She held out her ungloved hand and the horse sniffed it; she stroked his neck and spoke softly to him. His ears were pricked; he stood quietly, in no way bothered by his unusual rider.

She took the reins in one hand and swung onto the saddle. She expected to have to adjust the stirrup leathers but Albert had already done so. 'He's a fine beast, my lady. A bit lively, but none the worse for that. Might be best if I accompanied you this morning, just in case.'

'No, we'll be fine. He's no bigger than Sultan and I have no difficulty with him.' She settled into the saddle and clicked her tongue. The gelding moved off, mouthing his bit and sidling sideways in excitement. 'Calm down, my boy. You'll have your gallop soon, but first we need to get to know each other.'

After less than a quarter of an hour they were in perfect harmony, and she turned him towards the ride that encircled the park. This morning she wouldn't visit the folly; she must be back in her bedchamber in time to bathe. Whatever her feelings about her impending nuptials, she was determined not to let herself or her family down by appearing at anything less than her best.

After an exhilarating gallop she headed for the lower meadow, certain her mount would clear the ditches as easily as Sultan. Riding unencumbered by the long skirts of a habit was liberating; she was at one with her horse, and although he wasn't quite as responsive as her stallion, he came a close second.

There was one gate to negotiate. As she was using the bone handle of her crop to lift the rope that secured the gate to the fence post, someone called her name.

'Rosamond, wait there. I'll join you in a moment.' The duke was standing in his stirrups, looking over the hedge. He was smiling, and didn't appear in any way put out by her unorthodox appearance or the fact that she was astride his own horse. She had no time to reply as he vanished and urged his mount into a gallop. Her horse had heard his owner's voice and was dancing sideways, making it impossible to release the gate. Even if she had intended to ignore his wishes, she had no option but to remain where she was unless she attempted a risky jump.

A few minutes later he thundered into view. He was riding her stallion and looked as comfortable on him as she did on his gelding. He reined back and arrived at a more decorous pace.

'Good morning, sweetheart. Are you enjoying riding my horse?'

'I am, and are you enjoying riding mine?'

'Indeed I am, but I think it wise for us to exchange mounts. 'thello might misbehave now I'm here.'

She didn't argue. She was pretty sure she'd have no problems, but he was rescinding his instructions and that was all that mattered. He was dismounted before her and with his reins looped over his arm, reached up and lifted her from the saddle. He held her poised in mid-air so they were face-to-face and said in a conversational tone, 'Might I say, my dear, that I am somewhat surprised by your ensemble this morning?'

10

Rosamond didn't like the steely look in his eye. It hadn't occurred to her he would take issue with her riding astride in men's clothing when he'd joked about her stealing his horse. 'Your horse wouldn't go under a side-saddle so I had no choice. I always wear breeches under my habit anyway.' He lowered her to the floor but kept a firm grip on her arms.

'How true, my dear, and a perfectly sensible arrangement.' She began to breathe more easily and then he continued: 'However, at no time does anyone see said breeches. Today all the world has been treated, if that is the word, to the display of your derriere thrust into the air.'

'Now you're being ridiculous, Elliott. It's scarcely half past five and no one apart from you has seen anything they shouldn't.' She gave him glare for glare. 'Actually, I thought that as my riding coat covered me when I was on the ground, it would do the same when riding.'

'Did you indeed? Were you not aware, my love, that a *riding* coat is designed for ease of movement and therefore divides at the back?'

His dulcet tones and endearments didn't fool her for a moment. He was very angry indeed and justifiably so in the circumstances. There was nothing for it; she would have to apologise — not something she was fond of doing. 'I apologise for appearing in public inappropriately dressed. I give you my word it won't happen again.' For some reason her mouth carried on moving when she should have remained silent. 'None of this would have happened, sir, if I had been allowed to ride my own horse.'

She could almost hear his teeth grinding, but he made a valiant effort to cling onto the remnants of his temper.

The grip on her arms unexpectedly slackened and she took a step away. Her shoulders slumped and she shrugged and raised her hands as if in supplication. 'I don't know why I say such things to you when I know they will enrage you. Until two days ago I'd never been rude to anyone. In fact, I was always the one to step in and sort out any disputes.'

'And I don't know why I'm behaving like the worst kind of bully. We've both been behaving out of character. Believe it or not, Rosamond, I'm famous for being calm and slow to anger whatever the provocation.' He took her hands and raised them to his lips. She was held captive by his gaze and didn't snatch her hands away. With slow deliberation he kissed each knuckle in turn and her insides melted. What was happening to her? She swayed towards him and he released her hands in time to catch her, and for a second time her feet left the ground.

'Look at me, my love. I want to see your face.'

She wasn't sure she wanted to look at him. Keeping one arm firmly around her waist, he brought his other hand to her chin and gently tilted her head. Then the sun was blotted out as he lowered his head and covered her mouth with his own. His lips were firm and cold and were doing extraordinary things to her pulse. Her hands slid from his chest to link themselves in the soft black hair that curled at the nape of his neck.

Every inch of her was pressed hard against him and instead of being repelled by this intimacy, she revelled in it. His kiss was gentle and he seemed to be breathing into the very centre of her being. He abandoned her mouth and his lips trailed excitement in their wake as they moved from the corner of her mouth, down her cheek, until he was nuzzling behind her ear. She was almost faint with desire.

Then something heavy smacked her

in the middle of her back and Elliott lost his balance and they fell in a heap of arms and legs to the dew-soaked grass. Sultan's massive head nudged her, this time more gently. Laughing, she rolled over and scrambled to her feet.

'God's teeth, that was a close thing, sweetheart.' Elliott appeared to rise as if pulled by invisible strings, and his athleticism couldn't fail to impress her. He slapped the amiable stallion on the neck. 'Good lad, you intervened just in time.' Twin flags of colour stained his cheeks and he looked more flustered than she did by what had happened between them.

'I've never been kissed before, Elliott, and I must say it's a very enjoyable experience. I'd no idea . . . '

'So I should hope, and I must humbly beg your pardon for taking such shameful advantage . . . '

It was her turn to interrupt. 'Fiddle-sticks to that! Are we not to be married in a few hours' time? I believe we can do as we please from now on.' A look of such joy crossed his face that she didn't have the heart to retract her words. They both understood that things had changed irrevocably between them.

His voice was hoarse as he reached out and brushed an errant strand of hair from her cheek. 'I won't hold you to that, my darling, but if you have truly changed your mind about sharing my bed, then it's nothing short of the miracle I prayed for last night.'

The idea that someone so formidable could ask for God's intervention made him seem more vulnerable, less stern, and possibly a man who could make her an excellent husband. Heat pooled in a most unexpected place at the thought of what else they might share together, rather sooner than she'd thought.

'I believe that I might have changed my mind about . . . about . . . '

'Making love to me — is what you're trying to say?'

Scalding colour flooded from her

toes to her crown at his mention of something so intimate. Maybe she wasn't as ready as she'd thought to take the next step with a man she scarcely knew. Instead of laughing at her embarrassment, he briefly hugged her and kissed the top of her head. 'Don't worry, little one. We'll remain in our separate chambers until I'm certain you're ready to become my true wife.' He stopped and stared at her as if seeing her for the first time. 'Your mother has explained what takes place between a husband and wife in order to procreate children?'

This was a most unsuitable topic of conversation and she'd no wish to continue with it. She ducked under his arm and grabbed Sultan's reins. With her back firmly to him, she answered his question. 'No, it's not a conversation I've had with Mama, but I'm a country girl and have seen animals mating so have a fair idea of the process involved.'

He was behind her and she bent her

leg so he could toss her into the saddle. 'Excellent, but I can assure you it's a far more enjoyable process for humankind.' He pushed her leg forward in a matter-of-fact manner in order to adjust the stirrup leather whilst she did the same for her left leg. 'Were you intending to jump the ditches on my horse?'

'Of course — are you suggesting that I would have come to grief?'

'Absolutely not. As I've told you before, Rosamond dearest, you've the best seat in the kingdom.' He chuckled and squeezed her knee. 'Are we agreed that you'll refrain from showing the world your posterior in future?'

'As usual, sir, you're exaggerating the situation. At no time was *that* part of my anatomy visible to anyone — even you.' She looked down at him and his smile left her breathless. 'However, I promise I won't ride without my skirt in future.'

He swung into the saddle and moved his horse so they were adjacent. 'I notice you didn't promise not to ride astride — are you intending to repeat this outrage?'

'I sometimes ride astride, but if you object I'll not do it again.' She tapped him sharply on the knee with her crop. 'After all, I'm about to promise to honour and obey you for the rest of my life, am I not?'

'Words are easy to speak, my love, but actions are much harder.'

They took the easier route home, and as they approached he suggested she dismount. 'There will be a dozen stable boys and grooms working in the yard now. I'd prefer it if they didn't see you dressed like your brother.'

After his teasing remarks about her breeches, she was only too happy to comply. He was dismounted and at her side before she'd kicked her feet from the stirrups. She was beginning to enjoy being lifted as if she was a dainty Dresden miss and not a lanky, awkward beanpole of a girl.

'I must go in, but I promise I won't

keep you waiting.'

'My day is getting better by the minute.'

She was halfway up the back stairs before she understood his cryptic comment. She'd been referring to the wedding ceremony, he to what came afterwards. Although he had only arrived at Hathersage three days ago, she had spent more time alone with him than most young ladies did with their future husbands. He wasn't a stranger anymore; he was almost a friend, and very shortly would be her husband too. Perhaps his arrival had actually improved her life and not ruined it. If only her mother would come round, today could be most enjoyable.

Fortunately Jane was busy in the bathing room and Rosamond was able to remove her unsuitable attire without being discovered. A sumptuous spread had been set out in the sitting room — far more than she would usually consume for breakfast. Once safely in her robe, she hurried over to inspect what had been sent up for her.

Not only were there succulent slices of ham but also coddled eggs, toasted bread, and even a plate of Cook's delicious scones. These were not usually served in the morning, but Cook must have baked them especially because they were Rosamond's favourite.

After her invigorating ride and encounter with Elliott, she was ravenous. She piled her plate with ham and eggs and spread two pieces of toast thickly with butter. There was a full jug of chocolate, as well as another containing coffee. There was to be no formal wedding breakfast after the ceremony — in fact as far as she was aware, they would say their vows in front of the rector and then life would carry on as usual. As there were to be no guests, she supposed that was probably the best thing to do.

Her abigail arrived to announce the bath was ready just as Rosamond decided she couldn't eat another morsel. 'A long soak is exactly what I need.' She left her hair pinned securely to the top of her head.

'You wouldn't believe what's going on downstairs, my lady. The grand drawing room is being transformed for your wedding. His grace has all sorts of things arranged to make your day special.'

'I cannot imagine what, unless we now have dozens of wedding guests arriving.' She dropped her robe and stepped into the rose-scented water. 'I wonder how Mama managed before the baths were installed. Sitting with one's knees under one's chin in a hip bath in front of the fire just can't compare with the pleasure of stretching out full-length.'

'There's nobody coming from elsewhere as far as I know, my lady. However, all the indoor staff are to stand and watch, and afterwards there's to be a garden party with stilt-walkers and fire-eaters for everyone, including children and folk from the village. I've never seen the like. Your wedding day will be talked about for years to come, my lady.'

'I can't believe it; it doesn't seem credible that so much could be organised in so short a time. We only decided yesterday to be married this morning — how will all the villagers and tenants know about the event?'

'It only needs one person to take the message and then everyone will know within an hour. There's to be porter, lemonade and ale to drink as well as all manner of cold food put out on special tables. Word was that there will also be a hog roast — but I'm not certain about that.'

Mama had always forbidden any sort of gossiping with servants, but Rosamond had always considered Jane exempt from this rule. 'Have you heard if my apartment is to be vacated today?'

'That's another thing, my lady. Mrs Turner, a dozen indoor staff and several of the outside men have already transferred to the Dower House. They are to complete the improvements and have everything ready before we leave for Bath.' Jane was silent for a moment, obviously considering if it would be appropriate to mention anything further. 'Mr Gibson has said that Hathersage is to be put under holland covers and cleaned from top to toe in our absence. His grace has said that all the staff are to be given three days holiday in rotation as well.'

There was no need for Jane to say anything further. Elliott had played a masterly stroke by removing those members of staff who were loyal to her mother. Mama might see it as an olive branch, giving her the pick of the servants to run her new establishment. However, becoming the new mistress of Hathersage would be far easier without them.

'That's quite unprecedented — even Papa never granted extra leave above what they were owed.' She stepped carefully from the tub and Jane handed her a large bath sheet. 'No doubt he will be the most popular master in the neighbourhood after today.'

★　★　★

'Dammit, Jenkins, will you never be done with your fiddling?' Elliott heartily disliked being pampered by his valet, but today was different. He would only have one wedding day and wanted to look his best for his beautiful bride. One thing he was certain of: whether he had an heir or not, if anything ever happened to Rosamond he would never marry again. He closed his eyes and sent up a fervent prayer to the Almighty asking for his blessing and support, and also that his wife would outlive him.

'There, your grace. I'm done. Very smart you look, too, if I might be permitted to say so.' Jenkins stood back to admire his work.

'Are you quite sure I must wear this ridiculous gold sash? I'd much rather wear my sword.'

'The sash is part of your dress

uniform, your grace, and wearing a weapon to your wedding might upset the young ladies.'

'Is Lord Davenport ready? I wish to speak to him before he goes down.'

Elliott was pacing his spacious sitting room when his friend strolled in, looking equally magnificent in his scarlet regimentals. 'You wish to speak to me, Bromley? Here I am. What can I do for you?'

'Rosamond has no one to escort her this morning — would you do that for me?'

'I'd be delighted. I suppose you've heard nothing from the dowager? Do you think she'll swallow her pride and attend the wedding?'

'I hope she does, but I doubt she will. She must have been informed of my arrangements, and I'm hoping she'll see this in a positive light and not as a further attack on her dignity. Did I tell you? — I've had Dawkins draw up a settlement so that she's financially independent and doesn't have to come cap in hand to me to pay her bills. I've also had my man of affairs speak to her with regard to her particular requirements for her new home. There are going to be several bathing rooms installed, and both the kitchen and other offices are to be updated. I'm hoping that will be sufficient to bring peace to my new family.'

'You can do no more; I doubt that you and she will ever like each other, but for Lady Rosamond's sake, let's hope she'll put her personal animosity aside. Being married without either parent present will be a sad thing indeed.'

Elliott tugged at his gold frogged sash. 'I feel like a macaroni, but at least we're both rigged out in the same style. I was never comfortable in this uniform — too much gold — and I dislike intensely the over-decorated tails on the jacket.'

'You might dislike them, but I'm hoping Lady Amelia will be suitably impressed by the width of my shoulders, the solidity of my thighs in these skin-tight breeches and the high gloss to my boots. The ladies love an officer in scarlet — don't you recall the balls we attended with Wellesley? The civilian gentlemen were roundly ignored as soon as we marched in.'

'Time for you to present yourself at the rear of the house, and it's time for me to go downstairs and await my bride. Is everything in hand outside?'

Davenport nodded as he sauntered to the door. 'Was I not always an excellent adjutant? There will be entertainment, food and drink and perfect weather. With luck there might also be fireworks, but the pyrotechnic team haven't arrived as yet.'

Elliott had faced death in battle with less trepidation than he was feeling now. Was Rosamond as nervous as he? Hopefully she would have heard about his plans to celebrate the day and approved of them. As he turned to leave he came to a decision. Instead of exiting the sitting room, he returned to his bedchamber and knocked loudly on the communicating door. For a moment nothing happened, and then there was the sound of bolts being drawn back and a key being turned.

'Good morning, Duke. I was expecting you to call. Would you care to come in, or shall I join you in your apartment?' His future mother-in-law was smiling and this quite transformed her face. She was a trifle plump and her golden hair had faded a little, but now he could see she was still an attractive woman.

'If you would care to join me in my sitting room, madam, I should be delighted.' He smiled and stepped aside to allow her to proceed him. 'Might I say how elegant you look this morning, Duchess? Your gown is a very becoming shade of blue.'

She astonished him further by laughing. 'That's doing it rather too brown, sir. There is absolutely no need to pay me fulsome compliments. We have much to discuss and very little time in which to do it.'

11

Rosamond tilted her head and nodded. 'Yes, that's absolutely perfect, Jane. Thank you. The coronet of rosebuds looks spectacular, and I love the way you've arranged my hair. I'm beginning to feel like a real bride and not a sham.'

Her words were overheard by her sisters, who trooped in at that very moment. 'What do you mean? Of course you're a genuine bride. You will be a duchess in an hour's time, dear sister, and married to a very handsome gentleman. I almost wish we could change places.' Millie giggled and her cheeks coloured. 'However, I realised almost at once that *he* is not the one for me.'

Before she could comment there was a sharp knock on the door. Surely Elliott wouldn't come to see her now? A chambermaid scampered over to open the door and Lord Davenport strolled in. She was quite bowled over by his appearance. He was splendidly attired in his smart scarlet uniform with no end of gold frogging and dangling bits.

He bowed to her and nodded and smiled at her sisters. Millie blushed even more. So that was where the land lay — Davenport was a mere lord. It hadn't occurred to her that her sister might settle for anything less than an earl.

'Lady Rosamond, the duke has asked me to escort you to your wedding. He didn't wish you to walk the length of the grand drawing room alone.'

'I should be delighted to accept your kind offer, my lord, although I won't be alone as my sisters will be walking right behind me.'

He offered his arm and she placed her hand upon it. He was a very attractive gentleman, almost as handsome as Elliott. Millie handed her the pretty bouquet of rosebuds and greenery that exactly matched the flowers in her hair and the posies her sisters were carrying.

'I'm glad you all decided to wear similar gowns. The three of you look quite stunning in cream and white striped muslin.'

'Not as beautiful as you, Rosamond,' said Millie. 'I've never seen you in better looks, and I believe between us we selected the perfect outfit for such an auspicious occasion. You and the duke will make a very handsome couple.'

'Thank you. I sincerely hope he agrees with your assessment.'

Her escort patted her hand and smiled. 'He will be awestruck by your beauty, Lady Rosamond. I doubt anyone will ever see a more beautiful bride.'

She didn't believe his remark for one moment, but the comment was enough to settle her nerves and give her the much-needed confidence to begin the descent. Two footmen bowed her from her sitting room and two more were waiting to lead her down. As she crossed the gallery a delicious aroma wafted up to greet her. She wanted to run forward and peer over the balustrade, but today she must behave with absolute decorum.

Her breath caught in her throat as she saw what awaited her below. There were more than a dozen enormous vases of sweet-scented roses and summer flowers placed around the hall. Standing like guards of honour on either side of the vast space were the rest of the footmen, immaculate in their best livery. As they reached the bottom they bowed in unison.

She was moved almost to tears by the kindness and consideration of her future husband. She might not have one hundred guests to watch her marriage, but Elliott had made sure she would never forget this occasion. She smiled and blinked back tears as Davenport guided her expertly towards the open double doors of the grand drawing room.

A quartet struck up the wedding march as she arrived. How on earth had he found musicians so quickly? Then she was shocked as an unexpected figure moved from the shadows to stand beside her. 'Rosamond, I apologise for my bad behaviour. It was inexcusable. The duke has forgiven me and I sincerely hope you can find it in your heart to do the same.'

Rosamond forgot she was supposed to be composed and stately and threw her arms around her mother's neck, something she'd never done before. 'Mama, I can't tell you how pleased I am to see you here. Without this, today would have been a sad occasion. There's nothing to forgive.' The quartet continued to play and Davenport cleared his throat noisily. 'We shall talk after the service. Thank you so much for coming.'

They resumed their slow promenade into the huge chamber, which was now packed with smiling, happy people. The entire indoor staff appeared to be present down to the lowliest scullery maid. They stood in tidy rows and clean aprons on either side of the room. This chamber was also decorated with flowers and ribbons and smelled as sweet as the hall.

But she had eyes for nothing apart from the man who turned to face her at the far end of the room. Her eyes widened. She'd never seen anything so splendid as Elliott in his scarlet regimentals. He looked as stunned as she, and didn't take his gaze from her for a second as she glided down the polished parquet floor to stand beside him in front of the rector.

Davenport gently prised her hand from his arm and placed it on Elliott's waiting palm. 'You are breathtaking, my darling, and I'm the luckiest man in the world.'

'Mama is here. Now everything is going to be wonderful.' She should have acknowledged his compliment but always spoke from the heart. His smile made her bodice feel unaccountably tight and unexpected heat flashed around her body.

The musicians finished playing and Mama settled herself on the first of the single row of delicate gilt chairs (borrowed from the ballroom for today) on her left-hand side, and her sisters fluttered down beside her. Davenport and Dawkins were joined by Gibson and two unknown gentlemen on the right. A hush settled over the assembled audience and the rector beckoned them forward.

This was the first wedding she had attended, so the words were new to her, but she responded clearly and confidently when asked to. Elliott's strong baritone responses filled the room and left no one in any doubt he was speaking from the heart. She risked a glance in his direction and received a second scorching smile. Was it possible two people could fall in love on so short an acquaintance, or was it something else entirely that linked them?

She scarcely took in what was being

said, and when the rector pronounced them man and wife she could hardly credit it. Throughout the service Elliott hadn't released her hand, apart from the brief moment when he slipped the ring over her knuckle.

'Well, Rosamond, it is done. For better for worse, we're now man and wife, and I believe we must both learn the meaning of compromise.' He drew her closer and, ignoring the interested spectators, quite deliberately put his arms around her waist. Her hands moved of their own volition to encircle his neck. Her first kiss as his duchess was quite different from the previous ones. This time his mouth demanded a response, as if he was imprinting his possession before the witnesses. For a glorious few moments she was swept away and forgot everything — including the fact that her mother was sitting a scant yard from her.

The situation was saved by Gibson getting to his feet and calling for three cheers for the happy couple. Following this there was a spontaneous round of applause, and then she was being kissed and hugged by her sisters. Mama remained to one side, but actually looked pleased with what she saw. Had today worked a miracle with her mother as well? Would being the new duchess also make her feel part of the family and no longer the only daughter her mother disliked?

'Might I be the first to congratulate you both?' she said. 'I think you are ideally matched and will be very happy together. Rosamond, my dear, you will be delighted to know that your apartment will be vacant by this evening. I shall remove to the guest wing until my new home is ready. Hopefully that will be before everything is shrouded in covers.'

Rosamond was so overcome by her mother's loving expression that she forgot the years of unkindness and glanced at her husband. He immediately understood and nodded amiably. 'Mama, why don't you come with us to

Bath? I can remember you suggesting to Papa that we visit, but he could never be persuaded to leave Hathersage even for one night.'

'I should be delighted to accept your kind invitation, Rosamond, if you are quite sure your husband has no objection.'

'We would be honoured if you would agree to accompany us, Duchess. Indeed, how could a family holiday be successful without you there to keep us all in order?'

Rosamond was living in a dream where everything she'd ever wished for was coming true. She had married a wonderful gentleman who would take care of her and her family, and Mama was treating her in the same way as her sisters, which was all she'd ever wanted.

The rest of the day passed in a blur of excitement and happiness. She was surrounded by smiling faces and Elliott didn't leave her side for a moment. As dusk fell he led her inside.

'Well, my darling, I believe we can

say today was a success. Did you enjoy yourself?'

'I did — it has been the best day of my life. I'm astonished that you managed to organise so much in so short a time. Thank you, Elliott, for making our wedding day so wonderful.'

His smile made her toes curl in her slippers. 'There is one way you can thank me, sweetheart, but I won't be offended if you refuse.'

'There's something I need to explain to you, but not here. Somewhere private.'

'I'll come to your apartment in an hour. No, don't look so horrified. It won't be a conjugal visit, merely a companionable one.'

Her dresser was waiting in her new apartment. 'I've never been in this apartment, Jane. Not once was I invited, even though my sisters were often here. I'm not sure I'll be able to sleep in a place where I was never welcome.'

'That's as may be, your grace, but

today everything has changed. Hathersage is now your home, and you and his grace will decide how things are run in future.' Jane flushed and hastily dropped into a deep curtsy. 'I beg your pardon, your grace, for speaking out of turn.'

Although there'd been plenty of food on offer all day, Rosamond had been too excited to eat and was now regretting not sampling some of the treats. After she'd removed her lovely gown, completed her ablutions and slipped on her usual white cotton nightgown, she was almost tempted to send a chambermaid to the kitchen to fetch her a supper tray. Elliott had said he would come and the hour was almost up, so she must remain hungry.

The communicating door was closed, but she would never bolt it against him. He'd promised not to insist on sharing her bed until she was certain she wished him to, and his word was good enough for her. She curled up in the window seat and waited for a knock on the door. Jane and the girls had been dismissed; from the sniggering and nudging that took place they must think she was waiting for her husband for a quite different reason.

This chamber was so spacious that she wasn't able to hear anything from behind the door, so when a knock came she was startled. 'Come in; the door isn't locked.'

Elliott had also changed out of his uniform, but somehow she hadn't expected him to be in his robe. She also was astounded to see his manservant staggering behind him with a laden tray. 'Neither of us has eaten since this morning, so we'll have supper together whilst we talk.' He gestured towards a convenient side table and Jenkins put his burden down. He bowed and was gone before she could thank him.

'I'm beginning to think you have magical powers, Elliott. You seem able to anticipate my every wish. I'm starving and hope there's sufficient for both of us, as I'm famous for my prodigious appetite.'

They munched their way through the impromptu meal, discussing the high points of the day and laughing as they recalled the stilt-walker becoming entangled with his poles and falling headlong into the lake. When they were done he removed the tray and picked up a bottle of champagne.

'We have yet to toast our marriage, sweetheart. Will you drink a glass with me?' Not waiting for her answer, he deftly twisted off the cork with a satisfying pop and poured them each a glass of fizzy golden liquid.

'I've never tasted champagne. In fact, I doubt I've drunk more than half a dozen glasses of any sort of alcohol in my life.'

'Then only one glass for you, and I'll finish the bottle myself.'

They had eaten while sitting on cushions and he dropped beside her again without a drop of champagne spilling. 'The more I see of you, the better I'm impressed.' She accepted her glass and took a tentative sip. She smiled over the rim of her glass.

'However, I hope I've not married a drunkard, sir? Are you seriously intending to drink a whole bottle of champagne by yourself?'

He downed his glass in one gulp and refilled it immediately. 'Drink is the solace of the lonely, my darling. I fear I'll be obliged to consume vast quantities of alcohol whilst I'm obliged to sleep alone.'

She giggled and took a larger swallow of her drink, finding it more pleasant than she'd expected. 'Don't be ridiculous, and please don't drink yourself into a stupor until we've talked.'

Instantly he was alert, his expression watchful. 'Tell me. There's something bothering you, and I'm here to share your burdens in future.'

'This is very difficult for me to say, but there's something you need to know. Papa loved me; he never ignored me as my mother did. All my life I've prayed for her to show me some affection, and today was the first time that she did.' She took another mouthful of champagne while she gathered her thoughts. 'Initially I was delighted, but as the day progressed I've become suspicious of her *volte face*. Being pleasant to me is so out of character that I'm worried there might be more to it than we understand.'

'Forget her. The duchess no longer has any relevance to your life unless you wish her to. There's no barrier between you and your siblings, is there?' She shook her head and drained her glass. 'I thought not, and I'm eagerly anticipating launching them on an unsuspecting world. But you need see nothing of your mother. It's possible she was motivated by self-interest; for all her faults, she's not a stupid woman and will know on which side her bread is buttered.

'If she offends you then her offence to me is far worse, as I hold the purse strings. Well, actually that's no longer true. I've settled a substantial annuity on her, so she's actually an independent woman now.'

Absentmindedly he refilled her glass, drained his own and did the same with that. She didn't like the look on his face. 'Why are you looking so serious? Your kindness must be the reason she's decided to be pleasant to me.'

'I pray that's the case, but you've raised grave doubts in my mind. If she has some serious mischief in mind then I can no longer control her by financial means.' He shook his head and got up to stride around the room, cursing under his breath.

After a few minutes she decided to join him in his pacing, but not his cursing. She wasn't ready to use such language. She finished her drink and giggled. What a lot of rude words her husband knew! It must be because he was once a soldier. She attempted to get to her feet, but for some strange reason her legs refused to obey her. Her struggles attracted his attention.

'Good God! You should never have

had that second glass of champagne.' He leaned down and placed his hands around her waist. 'Up you come, my little inebriate. Time for bed.'

She breathed into his shoulder, loving his masculine scent of sandalwood and something she didn't recognise. 'I don't want you to be lonely. Stay with me; then you won't need to drink too much.'

'I've been asked to face some impossible challenges in my life, darling, but remaining with you tonight and not breaking my word is going to be the hardest.'

He flicked the sheet aside and placed her beneath it. Her head was feeling rather odd and she couldn't quite focus on him. Tenderly he covered her and then, as if he were about to lie on a bed of snakes, he lowered himself beside her. The bed dipped and she rolled closer so they were lying hip to hip. A delicious warmth engulfed her and she placed a hand on his bare chest, loving the roughness beneath her fingers.

'No, my love, not tonight. You're in

your cups and I'll not take advantage of you. When we make love I want you to be wide awake and certain of what you're doing.'

She sighed and snuggled against him. She was floating, relaxed and happy, but couldn't settle comfortably with her hair pinned up. 'My hair — can you remove the pins? Better with it down.'

'Sit up a little and I'll do it for you.'

Her pulse raced and her head spun as his fingers caressed her scalp. Then the weight on her head was gone as her hair tumbled over her shoulders. She was too tired to get out and plait it; tonight it must remain unbound. 'Thank you. Good night. I think I love you.' She closed her eyes and was instantly asleep.

12

Elliott was watching her hair cascade onto her shoulders when she murmured that she loved him. Her words pierced his heart and he was unmanned. He brushed aside his tears and gazed down at this beautiful young woman who inexplicably believed she was in love with him. He didn't deserve such happiness.

All his adult life he'd denied the existence of true love between mature adults — green boys and girls might imagine themselves so afflicted, but they soon grew out of it and understood that respect and affection were what cemented a marriage. Yesterday he'd realised he was wrong; love did exist and was as real as any other emotion. He was totally, irrevocably in love with his wife and had hoped one day to persuade her to feel the same.

Now, admittedly after too much champagne, she'd told him she loved him too.

With a shaking hand he stroked her glorious, softly waving hair. He couldn't imagine anything more lovely. He dipped his fingers into the silky tresses, finding them quite unlike anything he'd touched before. She was neither dark nor fair, but somewhere in between. He brushed a finger across her eyebrows — they were the exact match to her hair, whereas her lashes were long and dark and framed her fine eyes perfectly. These were sometimes green, sometimes golden brown — but always spectacular.

He couldn't remain next to her scantily clad body without wanting to make love to her. He ached to make her his, to show her how much he loved her, and that physical love could be a wonderful thing when the emotions were involved. He regretted his past liaisons with ladies of the *demimonde* and wished he could come to the marriage bed as pure and innocent as she.

He finished off the champagne and returned to his rooms to find the decanter of brandy he'd brought up from the study. If he drank this as well he could sleep beside her with no fear of doing something he'd regret for the rest of his life. He was infamous for being able to drink his comrades under the table, but for some reason tonight it only required one glass of brandy to push him from sober to disguised.

Normally he slept naked, but tonight he thought it wise to keep his silk robe wrapped firmly round him. The night was warm, but not unpleasantly so; just right for sleeping without a cover. He stretched out beside the girl he'd give his life for, gathered her close to his heart and fell deeply asleep.

He was roused by the entrance of a maid who took one look and fled the room. Chuckling to himself, he pushed away the curtain of hair that was covering his beloved and kissed her awake.

'Darling, we must rise. We have important papers to sign so Dawkins can release the care of the duchy into my hands.' Her glorious eyes flickered open and she yawned and stretched.

'I have a shocking headache, husband. Is that from drinking champagne with you?'

'And I, wife, have a mouth like a bear pit and my headache is far worse. We are a disgrace, there's no doubt about it. By the way, the chambermaid came in a moment ago and ran away with her apron over her head.'

'Why should she do that? What did you say to shock her?' She smiled and it took all his self-control not to take her in his arms and make love to her.

'Nothing, my love, but I fear she saw rather more of my anatomy than she'd expected. I've nothing on beneath this robe, you know.'

She blushed a delightful shade of beetroot and hid her face under the sheet. 'Go away and get dressed and I shall do the same.' Her words were muffled but he understood her well enough.

'Put on your habit, darling. We'll ride after the documents are dealt with and breakfast on our return.'

*   *   *

Rosamond remained hidden until she was quite certain he'd left the room and closed the door behind him. To think that he'd been beside her with almost nothing on and she'd not realised it. She wasn't sure if she was disappointed or relieved that he'd kept his word. Her head was pounding and she didn't feel at all well. She toppled out of bed and steadied herself against the bedpost. She wasn't sure she had the energy to get up today, but Elliott would probably drag her out of bed if she remained there.

Jane bustled in to inform her there was hot water for her morning wash waiting in the bathing room. Once she was on the move her stomach settled and her head wasn't so painful. As she was riding, her choice of outfit was simple — the green or the gold. Elliott hadn't seen the latter, so she chose that one.

She was glad there was no plan to eat until later, as she didn't think food would be a good idea at the moment. If the result of imbibing too much alcohol was so unpleasant, why on earth did so many gentlemen drink to excess? No doubt she would understand these things in time.

She was sorely tempted to slide down the banister as he had on the day of his arrival. She could hardly believe that was only four days ago — five days ago they had expected Millie to become the new duchess. She stopped so suddenly that her toes were crushed against the end of her riding boots. Her heart pounded and for a horrible moment she thought she would cast up her accounts.

Last night as she'd been drifting off to sleep she was certain she'd told Elliott that she loved him. Could this feeling that she was going to explode with happiness, that her feet were several inches from the floor, be love? In the books she'd read, and the two books she'd written, the hero and heroine hadn't discovered their true feelings until half-way through the story. Was real life actually more exciting than fiction?

Her husband strolled into view and she caught her breath. It didn't matter she'd known him for less than a week; she loved him and wanted to be his true wife. She smiled and his eyes darkened and he pounded up the stairs to lift her from her feet. 'Darling, I love you to distraction and if we didn't have that wretched lawyer waiting for us I would take you back to bed this very minute and show you exactly how much.'

'I love you too. I don't know how it happened, but I'm bursting with excitement and joy.'

They were so engrossed in each other

that she wasn't aware they were being observed until he tensed and slowly returned her to her feet. He kept his arm tightly around her and slowly turned her round.

'Duchess, good morning. I trust you slept well in your new accommodation.' Mama was never abroad before noon, so something must have got her from her bed.

'Adequately. I have decided not to accompany you to Bath but leave immediately for an extended stay with friends.' She nodded and her lips curved but her eyes weren't smiling.

Rosamond pressed closer to Elliott; she was used to seeing her mother look straight through her or stare at her with dislike, but this was something else entirely. Her mother's expression was malevolent.

'You are free to do as you please, madam. Unfortunately there are no carriages available for your journey, but I'm sure you will be perfectly comfortable travelling by post-chaise.'

Her eyes sunk further into her plump cheeks and her nostrils flared. 'So be it. I had intended to pass on some pertinent information in private, but in the circumstances you will understand why I wish to tell you immediately.'

Elliott was beside Mama before she'd finished speaking and half-lifted her off her feet and bundled her into the nearest room. Rosamond followed him and slammed the door shut behind them.

Even enraged as she was, her mother remained dignified and didn't struggle. He strode to the furthest corner of the room, as far away from any eavesdroppers as he could, before putting her down. 'Now, madam, feel free to speak. There's nothing you can tell us that will alter anything. So do your worst — believe me, I intend to do the same.'

He held out his hand and Rosamond took it. He squeezed it and drew her to his side. She wanted to sit down to hear whatever dreadful news her mother had; she didn't think her legs would support her for much longer. He murmured softly, for her ears alone. 'Courage, sweetheart. Don't give an inch, whatever you hear. I love you and nothing will come between us, I give you my word.' They turned to face this person who was no longer a mother but an enemy.

'I had an affair with a house guest when the duke was away on business. You, Rosamond, are the product of that liaison — you are an illegitimate baby that my husband decided on a whim to bring up here. You, Duke, have married a bastard, and be very sure that everyone in society will soon be aware of this. You will be shunned and ridiculed throughout the country.'

Whatever she'd expected to hear, it had not been something as appalling as this. The man who'd loved and protected her had not been her real father, just a kind man taking care of the child produced by his unfaithful wife. Her life was ruined, but Elliott's need not be.

With great dignity she moved away from him, finally understanding why this woman had rejected her all her life. 'You are mistaken, madam. His grace will remain untainted by my shame. Our marriage shall be annulled. I am still a maiden — if you had waited to spit your vitriol until tomorrow you would have succeeded.' She couldn't look at her erstwhile husband; didn't want to see the look of disgust on his dear face at being trapped in a marriage with someone impossible.

She would leave this place immediately — she had no right to remain at Hathersage. The walk to the village was no more than two miles and could be accomplished in an hour. A coach departed for London at midday; with luck there would be an inside seat for her.

As she walked stiffly from the room she prayed he might call her back; that despite her being the daughter of an unknown father, he would stand by her. He said nothing and she walked out of the door and out of his life forever. Misery weighed her down and something as simple as placing one foot in front of the other was almost impossible. She would not break down — must remain in control — or she would never be able to organise her packing and depart for the village.

Her apartment was empty; her servants were no doubt downstairs breaking their fast. She would have liked to say farewell to Jane, but it would be easier this way. Quickly she stripped off her habit and tossed it aside — as usual she had her breeches on and decided to wear them. One day she might have need of them and it would be far easier to wear them than to carry them in her bag.

She pulled on the plainest of her gowns, one in moss-green cambric that had a matching pelisse, and modest chip-straw bonnet. Her riding boots remained on her feet, but she pushed two pairs of slippers and her walking boots into the corners of her valise. She hastily rolled up petticoats and stockings before adding another green gown, this one in Indian cotton, and a heavier grey dress that she'd worn to mourn her father.

She lifted the bag to test its weight and thought she could add a spare pair of gloves and a shawl and spencer. This left a small space for her writing materials and journal. She fastened the carpet bag and placed it ready by the hidden door. She glanced at the mantel clock — little less than a quarter of an hour had passed since her life had fallen apart and her heart had been smashed to pieces. She wasn't going to wait to be sent packing, but would leave with her head held high. None of this was her fault; she'd done nothing wrong apart from being born out of wedlock.

All she needed was to collect her purse, in which there were half a dozen gold sovereigns; more than enough to pay her lodgings somewhere anonymous in London until she found employment in a house somewhere. She was too young to apply to be a governess but thought she could pass herself off as a lady's maid. She would write herself a reference from the Duchess of Hathersage — after all, until the marriage was dissolved she was still that person.

Sultan and Calli must remain here. The duke would take care of them and they would soon forget her, as would her half-sisters. Millie must marry his grace now, and even if she were invited to stay as a poor relation, she couldn't remain in the same house and see him married to someone else. She was about to leave when she decided it might make things easier if her disappearance remained undiscovered until after the coach left.

How could she achieve this? If she locked all the doors then his grace (she was no longer entitled to refer to him less formally) would think her prostrate with misery and humiliation and leave her to recover her composure. She pushed the bolster under the sheets and drew the bed hangings. As long as Jane didn't approach too closely, it looked as though a figure was huddled there. There was one last thing to do: remove her wedding band and place it in a prominent position on the dressing table.

She forced everything from her mind and ran down the back stairs and slipped through the side door without being seen. There was a short cut through the woods to the village which she would take, as this would keep her from being seen on the lane that led from Hathersage Hall to the village with the same name.

What should she call herself? She was no longer a member of the aristocracy, and not entitled to use Hathersage anymore. She must devise a new persona, start again and try and forget she had ever been Lady Rosamond or the beloved wife of a duke.

★　★　★

Elliott waited until Rosamond had gone before opening his attack. He wanted to throw the venomous creature headfirst through the window and barely restrained himself from doing so. He would deal with the woman and then comfort his wife. 'I don't give a damn what you say or to whom you say it. Whatever you do, Rosamond will remain the Duchess of Hathersage and you will remain a ruined woman. You betrayed your husband and he forgave you and took your daughter to his heart.

'He could have had her fostered, have had you cloistered somewhere, but instead he continued to love you and the wonderful girl you rejected.' He didn't raise his voice; he'd no need to, as his expression was enough to make her shrivel. 'How someone as repellent as you managed to produce four delightful daughters is quite beyond me. I shall do what your husband didn't. I shall have you removed from here and incarcerated in a small and unpleasant estate in Northumbria. You will receive no visitors and will remain there until you die, which cannot come soon enough for me — the world will be well rid of you.'

His words whipped across the room, each one like a physical blow. He was unmoved to see her disintegrate before him, change from a confident woman to a snivelling heap. He added one last threat. 'You will reveal nothing of this, madam, if you wish to reach your destination safely.' He thought she promised she wouldn't say a word but her words were indistinct, disguised by her snuffles and sobs. He had no sympathy for her; she deserved everything he'd heaped upon her miserable head.

The first part of his job was done; now he must complete the second. Davenport could escort the woman; she could take a handful of personal servants and whatever luggage she'd packed. However, no jewellery or money would go with her. He'd allow her no access to funds, no opportunity to spread her venom even through letters.

He found his friend downstairs talking to the lawyer. He quickly apprised them both of what had transpired and they were as shocked and horrified as he had been.

'God damn it, Bromley, that woman should be horsewhipped. I'll be happy to take her wherever you say and make sure she's suitably miserable on the journey.'

Dawkins nodded his agreement. 'I concur, your grace. By so doing this information will be kept secret, at least for a few years. By then you will have established yourselves and hopefully have a nursery full of children. There might be a scandal of sorts, but I doubt that it will make any difference to you and your family. Fortunately, your grace, I've not yet processed the documents relating to the dowager's trust fund, so I'll burn those immediately.'

He nodded. 'I'll take care of the

details for this transfer, your grace, and will also arrange for the release of funds immediately so all bills can be paid. Might I ask you to you sign these documents before you leave?'

'Of course. My wife can sign tomorrow when she's feeling more the thing. I thank you, Dawkins. I knew I could rely on your discretion. I must speak to Gibson and get him to set things in motion — he'll know who to send with her.'

He shook hands with his friend and nodded to the lawyer. 'I am in your debt. I'll not forget your help today.'

'My pleasure, old fellow. I'll get my man to pack my trappings and will be ready to ride within the hour.'

The butler appeared at the door. 'Gibson, the dowager will be leaving immediately for Northumbria. Lord Davenport will be escorting her. I wish you to select four servants to accompany her, and have ready my travelling carriage, and another for the servants and the luggage. Both carriages will return, but the servants will not.'

'The luggage is already downstairs and her grace has chosen those she wishes to accompany her. Everything you request will be done within half an hour.' He bowed solemnly and backed out, loyal to the back bone, as were the rest of the staff. Elliott was confident no one had overheard what had been said. Now all that remained was for him to sign the papers and find his beloved girl and put things right.

His darling had worshipped her father and this morning that relationship had been destroyed. He would explain it made no difference to him who her parents were, or if he ever set foot in London again: she was his duchess and his soulmate. His eyes filled whilst he was signing the documents. If he hadn't already loved her to distraction, after her courageous performance, he would certainly love her now. Without hesitation she'd set him free; was prepared to face anything in order to ensure he was not tainted by association.

He rubbed his eyes and his pulse quickened. He was going to make love to her, consummate their union, then the marriage would stand whatever her objections.

13

The walk to the village seemed considerably longer than the two miles Rosamond knew it to be. She'd not travelled more than half a mile when her dog arrived at her side. 'No, Calli, you can't come with me. Go home, home, boy.' Her dog whined and pressed himself against her, unwilling to leave. 'Home. Go. Do as you're told.' She snapped her instruction and he slunk off. She remained looking down the path until she was certain he'd obeyed.

She resumed her journey, trying not to give in to tears. Her boots were designed for riding and long before she reached the destination her legs were hot and uncomfortable. She was grateful they were a comfortable fit so she wouldn't have blisters to contend with as well.

By concentrating on her physical discomfort she was able to force the black despair away; this would overwhelm her if she allowed it to. Halfway to Hathersage village she realised her plan was fatally flawed. How could she buy a ticket on the common stage when everyone had seen her become the Duchess of Hathersage only yesterday?

She had no option; she would have to avoid it and continue to cut across country until she reached the toll road. There was a busy coaching inn where she was sure she was less likely to be recognised. If necessary she could overnight at this establishment. She had more than enough in her reticule to cover her travelling expenses.

Perhaps if she found somewhere to sit down she could change into her walking boots and somehow squash her riding boots into the carpetbag in their place. The fastenings bulged alarmingly after she'd completed this procedure, but at least she was now comfortable and sure she could walk the extra miles.

Her active lifestyle had been a constant source of irritation to her mother, but now Rosamond was thankful she'd ignored the barbed comments and kept herself healthy and fit.

When she eventually reached her destination she was delighted to discover the mail coach to London was expected at any moment. She bought her ticket and had time to drink a welcome mug of porter and visit the privy before the vehicle trundled over the cobbles and halted outside. The passengers inside weren't allowed to alight at this stop and those waiting to board were encouraged to scramble on as quickly as possible.

The horses were changed, the mail collected, and the coach ready to leave in less than ten minutes. Rosamond found herself squashed between a sleeping, portly matron with a smelly lapdog, and an equally large gentleman who was clutching a basket of what sounded suspiciously like poultry. She wasn't sure which was the most malodorous and could only hope that one or the other weren't travelling all the way to London. There was no time to examine the other occupants as the coach rocked forward.

She pushed her precious bag behind her legs and tried to breathe through her mouth. The coach rumbled from the yard and out onto the smoother toll road. Never having travelled in such a way before, she was surprised how little room each passenger was allowed.

However hard she tried, she couldn't prevent her knees from bumping those of the person opposite — thank goodness this was a young woman and not a gentleman. Loud snores came from the man next to her and from the one in the far corner; hopefully they would sleep and not wish to talk to her. An elderly woman dressed entirely in black was in the fourth corner and she too was asleep, but silently, unlike the others.

Rosamond risked a glance across the coach and was greeted by a friendly smile. 'It's a bit of a squash, but cheap and reliable. Are you going all the way?' The young woman spoke with the diction of a gentlewoman. Her attire was of good quality but unfashionable. Maybe she was a governess on her way to a new position.

'I am; do you have any idea at what time I'll arrive in London tonight?'

'By six — if you're not delayed on the way in.' She offered her hand. 'I am Claire Browning.'

Rosamond needed to come up with a suitable name. 'And I am Mary Jamieson. I'm delighted to meet you, Miss Browning.'

They shook hands and an immediate rapport was formed. 'Are you visiting friends in town, Miss Jamieson?'

'I wish that were the case, Miss Browning, but unfortunately my circumstances have changed and I'm obliged to seek employment.'

'My great aunt who lives in Guildford has broken her leg, and my father is sending me to take care of her. I'm dreading the visit, as she's a most cantankerous old lady, and nothing I do will satisfy her.'

'I thought I might seek a position as a companion. I believe there are agencies one can visit in order to find employment of this sort.'

'Please, Miss Jamieson, postpone your search and come with me. The house is vast and Aunt Agatha too parsimonious to employ sufficient staff to keep it comfortable. The only thing that makes a visit bearable is that she has an excellent cook.' The young lady smiled encouragingly. 'Does the fact that you can see the castle from the house make my suggestion more tempting?'

Without hesitation Rosamond accepted this extraordinary offer. The Almighty was indeed taking care of her today and had sent Miss Browning to help her. 'Are you quite sure? I'm a complete stranger to you and might be a notorious criminal on the run from the magistrates.'

Her new friend spluttered and could barely contain her merriment. 'I'm prepared to take that chance, Miss Jamieson. I don't believe there are many villains who dress as well as you do, or wear such a fetching bonnet.'

'If you will forgive me, Miss Browning, I'm finding the motion of this vehicle is making me feel rather unwell and it might be best if I concentrate on not disgracing myself.' This was pure fabrication, but she just couldn't continue the light-hearted conversation when with every minute that passed she was further away from the man she loved, and the only home she'd ever known.

* * *

Too much time had passed since Rosamond had run out of the room; she must believe that Elliott abandoned her, and he wouldn't blame her. He was certain once he'd explained the whole situation, she would understand his reasons for not coming to her immediately. Jenkins was elsewhere and his own apartment empty. He knocked softly on the communicating door and waited for her reply. There was none. He rapped again, this time with more vigour.

'Sweetheart — Rosamond — I'm coming in. I must talk to you.' He turned the knob but the door didn't budge. He put his shoulder to it and pushed — still no movement.

Why had she locked him out? The hair on the back of his neck rose and he had a sinking feeling in his gut.

He didn't bother to try the other doors but shot through the exit Jenkins used and found his way to the door her servants used. He burst through into a small room in which three girls were sitting quietly, sewing. He ignored them and rushed through into Rosamond's bedchamber.

At first glance there seemed to be a sleeping figure behind the curtains, but he knew better. He threw them back and, as he'd feared, Rosamond was not there. For a second the pain of her disappearance held him immobile. Then his soldier's brain took over.

The three girls were staring, white-faced and stunned by his revelation. He pointed to the oldest. 'Are you Jane?' The girl nodded and stepped forward, dipping in a brief curtsy. 'Your mistress has gone. Check her closet and see what she's taken and tell me what you think she'll be wearing. Don't stand there gawping — do it now.' His sharp command had the desired effect and the girl gathered her wits and ran into the closet.

He looked around to see if she'd left a note and saw instead the glint of her gold wedding band. God in his heaven! She had believed her own nonsense and run away. She couldn't have got far; she would be on foot and carrying a bag. Her maid returned.

'There's only one bonnet missing, your grace, so her grace must be wearing a moss-green gown and matching pelisse.

247

As far as I can see only a grey gown, and another one in green, are missing.'

'Excellent — well done. Don't look so worried; I'll return your mistress by the end of the day.'

Thank God he was already suitably dressed for riding. He removed sufficient funds from his bureau drawer to cover every eventuality and was ready to depart. He took the stairs three at a time and the footman barely had time to fling open the front door as he raced towards it. He arrived in the stable yard to find Sultan saddled and waiting for him.

'This beast will find his mistress for you. He'll not let you down, your grace.'

There was no time to ask how word of Rosamond's disappearance had already arrived in the stable yard, but he was grateful it had. He swung into the saddle and pushed the stallion into a gallop before his feet were firmly placed in the stirrup irons. He was barely halfway down the drive when the unmistakable sound of a second horse made him rein back a little.

Davenport cantered alongside him, his expression grim. 'A damnable business, Bromley. I'll be better with you, than escorting the dowager to Northumbria. Your man of business has taken my place. We were about to leave when I heard your wife was missing.'

'I'm glad you're with me. It's just possible she'll still be walking to the village and we can end this nightmare right away.'

Conversation was impossible at the speed they were travelling and he concentrated on pushing his horse faster, praying he would find her before she boarded a coach. Removing her from that in front of the other passengers would cause the very scandal he was hoping to avoid. He didn't give a damn for society's opinion, but he had three sisters to launch and word of Rosamond's illegitimacy would ruin any chance of the girls making advantageous marriages.

They were approaching the outskirts of the village and he didn't wish to draw unnecessary attention by arriving pell-mell. Now they were trotting side by side, they were able to resume their conversation. 'Davenport, if this gets out will you withdraw your interest from Millie?' The fury on his friend's face at this suggestion made an answer redundant. 'I beg your pardon. That was maladroit of me. Like me, you don't give a damn for the ton; you'll marry her whatever happens.' He managed a slight smile. 'Mind you, we don't know that she'll have you yet.'

The coach yard was empty — he was too late. An ostler approached him and tugged his forelock. 'Are there any passengers waiting inside for the next stagecoach?' Elliott asked.

'No, your lordship, there ain't no one.' The man added nothing else.

'Did any passengers board?'

'No, your lordship, no tickets sold today.'

Elliott tossed the man a couple of

coins and headed for the road. 'She didn't come here, so where the hell has she gone? I've not thought this through properly. I should have discovered if she has friends in the area she might have gone to.'

'Not likely to have stayed in the neighbourhood, Bromley. She'll want to go somewhere she's not known.'

'Buggeration! Rosamond wouldn't have come here; she would have gone to the toll road. There must be a way across country that will save us time. Give me a moment; I need to get my thoughts in order . . . I believe she'll already be on the coach, but we can travel much faster than that. I intend to be at the next halt to collect her. She'll have to ride pillion, but I don't suppose she'll mind.'

'Are you sure about that? She might refuse to come with you, let alone return in such an undignified way. I thought the object was to avoid drawing attention to what's happened.'

'I don't give a damn about that

anymore, but you're right, we need a carriage. Davenport, will you go back to Hathersage and arrange for a closed carriage to meet me at Guildford? I'll arrange for a room in which we can wait, but ensure my staff are aware we'll be back before dark.'

'Do you know where you're going? If you intend to overtake the coach you'll have to take a shortcut, and you're not familiar with this country.'

'I know my north from my south and will have no difficulty taking a cross-country route. Thank you for your assistance, Davenport, and hopefully I'll see you later on today.' He grinned. 'No, make that tomorrow. I shall be busy tonight on other matters.'

Things were not as bleak as he'd first thought. He was confident he could persuade Rosamond there was no need for her to be a martyr. One thing was certain: after tonight the marriage wouldn't be in name only.

* * *

The coach made excellent time, as the road was dry and no passengers needed to alight or board at the next stop. Collecting the mail took only a few minutes, and soon they were bowling along towards Guildford. This was a market town Rosamond visited once or twice with her father, a place of steep cobbled hills and a half-ruined castle.

Would Elliott have discovered her absence? No doubt he would be relieved he didn't have the distasteful task of asking her to leave. The lawyer was in residence and could immediately set in motion the annulment, and with luck he would be free to marry again within a few months.

The thought of him being married to someone else was tearing her apart; even knowing it would be her oldest sister who took her place didn't make things easier. She kept her head dipped so the brim of her bonnet hid her face; she didn't want her new companion to see how wretched she was. If Miss

Browning knew why she was running away, the invitation would be instantly withdrawn.

Perhaps she should continue to London as planned, but travelling so far on her own was a daunting prospect. She would be much happier somewhere she was familiar with. Although Papa had been the leading landowner in the county, she was pretty sure no one would recognise her as his daughter, as she'd been a schoolroom miss when she'd accompanied him all those years ago.

'Miss Jamieson, we shall be arriving very shortly.'

Rosamond quickly wiped her eyes and straightened her bonnet. 'I shall be relieved to be on terra firma, Miss Browning. I'd forgotten how much I disliked travelling by stage.' As this was the first time she'd been obliged to take the mail coach, this was a deliberate fabrication — certainly the first of many falsehoods if she was to maintain her deceit.

She stepped from the coach, making sure she was unobserved by either coachman. With luck they would not even notice she'd got off before the destination she'd paid for, and this would make any search for her more difficult. She staggered and only remained upright because her companion grabbed her round the waist. 'Are you still feeling poorly, Miss Jamieson? You do look rather unwell. My great aunt lives adjacent to the castle. Do you think you can manage to walk that far?'

'I can indeed, thank you. I'll be perfectly fine once I've been in the fresh air for a while.' They crossed the busy road and took a narrow path which led to the top of the hill. Rosamond had no need to hide, as nobody would be looking for her.

Miss Browning stopped at a large wooden gate set in a six-foot wall. 'We shall go in this way. It will be unbolted for me, but we must fasten it behind us.'

The garden was substantial, far bigger and far grander than Rosamond had expected. The yew hedges were neglected and the lawns a trifle unkempt, but the overall impression was of wealth and substance. The house was four storeys high with a dozen or more windows overlooking the garden, and there was also a glasshouse and large vegetable pottager.

She'd been expecting something more modest; a girl who travelled unaccompanied on the mail coach could hardly come from a wealthy family. There was something decidedly odd about all this and she began to regret her impulsive decision to accompany this stranger.

'I know what you're thinking, Miss Jamieson. You're wondering why I should be obliged to travel as I did, are you not?'

Rosamond blushed. 'I must be honest; that's exactly what I was thinking. Your great aunt is obviously a wealthy woman — '

'And I am obviously not. Great Aunt Agatha is my mother's aunt; my father is a curate and Mama married beneath her. For all her faults, Aunt Agatha has been a godsend over the years, whereas the rest of the family have cut Mama off completely.'

'It's really none of my business, Miss Browning, and thank you for being so frank.' She stopped on the flagstone path that ran around the house. 'I must tell you that I've not been completely honest with you. I am indeed looking for employment, but I'm not Miss Mary Jamieson.' Her throat thickened and for a moment she couldn't continue. 'I've no idea who I am. I discovered this morning that I am the bastard child of an unknown father and not the well-bred young lady I always thought I was. It's for that reason I was on the coach. I could no longer remain somewhere I didn't belong.'

'I guessed it might be something like that. Remain Miss Jamieson; it's as good a name as any. Won't you call me Claire? I dislike intensely being referred to as Miss Browning.'

'Thank you. My given name is Rosamond — at least of that I'm quite sure.' She had been about to offer her hand, but her new friend embraced her instead. 'Exactly what are you going to tell your aunt? Will she not be perplexed by you arriving with a complete stranger at your side?'

'I shall tell her you're a school friend whose visit could not be postponed; therefore you agreed to accompany me and offer any assistance you could.'

'How ingenious! Does this school we both attended have a name?'

'Aunt Agatha won't bother to ask. She'll accept what we tell her and think she's lucky to have two young ladies at her beck and call, instead of one.' Claire took Rosamond's arm. 'I'm rather dreading going in. I don't suppose we'll be allowed to see the light of day for weeks — Aunt Agatha will keep us running about indoors.'

'In which case, why not give me a tour of the garden before we go inside? I don't suppose arriving a quarter of an hour later than expected will do any harm?'

14

Elliott saw the mail coach turn into the yard from the private parlour he'd reserved. He tossed the newspaper he'd been reading to one side and strode out to collect his errant wife. Rosamond would alight here like all the rest and he could whisk her into the parlour without anyone being aware of it.

He watched the influx of eager passengers heading for the snug, scanning the group for his beloved. They would have half an hour to eat before bundling back to the coach ready for the next stage. He waited, but she didn't appear. Perhaps she'd remained on the coach, too miserable to join the others for a communal meal.

The coach was empty. One of the coachmen was in the yard, so he accosted him. 'I was meeting a passenger — a young lady. But she doesn't appear to be here.'

The man touched his cap with his whip. 'No, my lord, she ain't. The young lady what had a ticket for Guildford has already left.'

'Were there any other young ladies on the coach today?' The man might think he was a depraved creature on the prowl for any available young woman. He dropped a silver sixpence into the man's hand and this had the desired effect.

'There was another one, going all the way to London, my lord. I reckon as she's inside with the others.'

'Thank you. I shall make further enquiries from the landlord.' He could hardly barge into the snug and start questioning the passengers himself, but he could send someone else in to ask for him.

He ducked his head on the way in and in the gloomy interior saw a stout matron clutching a ridiculous dog heading in his direction. He stepped in front of her and bowed deeply. 'I beg your pardon, madam. Could you spare me a few moments of your valuable time?'

'Certainly, sir. How can I help you?'

'I temporarily mislaid a member of my family. I'm certain she took a seat on the mail coach, but she appears to have vanished. I'm hoping you might shed some light on this.' He gave her his most charming smile and she simpered like a debutante.

'Indeed I can, sir. Miss Jamieson, the person you're looking for, struck up a friendship with another young lady who has gone to stay with her Great Aunt Agatha in a house near the castle.' His informant nodded and smiled. 'The aunt has broken her leg and Miss Browning is going to look after her.'

'Thank you, madam. That has been extraordinarily helpful. Permit me to say what a delightful dog you have there — an ideal companion for a handsome woman like yourself.' He bowed again and retreated into the coach yard before she could thrust the smelly object into his arms.

Finding the castle would be no problem, for he could see it across the road, looming from the top of the hill. It shouldn't be beyond him to locate the house in question; there couldn't be many elderly ladies in the vicinity with the first name of Agatha and who had a niece called Browning.

He would make some judicious enquiries before knocking on any doors. He waited for a gap in the traffic and then crossed and took a winding cobbled lane to the top of the hill. There were only three substantial properties adjacent to the castle, which narrowed down his search somewhat. He saw an urchin and beckoned him over. The boy was only too happy to point out the house he wanted in exchange for a coin.

★　★　★

The tour of the garden completed, Claire decided they could delay no longer and led Rosamond to a side door. She gestured to a red brick building they hadn't investigated. 'That's the coach house and stables. An archway leads from the lane outside into the yard. As there are no horses here, there's nothing much to see.' She stopped at a door. 'Aunt Agatha prefers us to use this entrance. The front door's just for important visitors.' She smiled. 'Not that there are any of those — my aunt has managed to offend all the neighbours, so no one comes anymore.'

Only then did Rosamond notice her new friend was not carrying any luggage. 'My goodness, you've left your bag behind.'

'No, I haven't. I keep a selection of garments here, as I'm frequently summoned for one reason or another. Mama is hopeful I'll be the sole beneficiary when Aunt Agatha goes to meet her maker — but I think it more likely she leave it to the church or some other charity.'

The door opened into a narrow

passageway, which had an unpleasant aroma Rosamond couldn't quite place. The floor was unpolished and her heart sank. Claire had warned her that this house was understaffed, and its neglect was obvious. She had a nasty suspicion she would be more parlour maid than companion over the next few weeks.

'I know what you're thinking, but you're wrong. Even my aunt wouldn't dream of asking either of us to clean the house; on this occasion I'm actually needed to fetch and carry, but usually my role is merely as companion. I believe I'm the only relative or friend who can remain in her company without becoming permanently offended.'

'She must be a termagant; I'm shaking in my boots at the thought of what she might say to me, turning up unannounced as I have.'

'I never let her bully me. I remain scrupulously polite but always reply in kind. Actually, I think she enjoys the cut and thrust of our conversations.' Claire led them into a spacious vestibule and pointed to the stairs. 'Why don't you put your valise down there; I'll show you where you're sleeping later. I'm afraid we'll have to make the bed ourselves — but there's plenty of linen and more than enough bedrooms. We must brave the lioness in her den before we do that.'

The entrance hall was reasonably clean — not as pristine as at Hathersage, but then nothing would ever compare favourably with her previous home. Rosamond could hardly credit how her life had changed in the past week. She had met, married and fallen in love with an extraordinary gentleman and then, like Cinderella after the ball, was now a girl with no name and no future.

'That's strange. Do you hear that?' Claire frowned as she stopped outside the double doors that must lead to the drawing room. 'I'm almost certain there's someone in there with my aunt.'

She stepped closer and pressed her

ear to the door. 'Yes, there's definitely someone in there. The rector must be making his monthly visit. How unfortunate. I think it would be better if you don't come in with me. I'll take you upstairs and you can choose a room and make a start on the bed. Don't look so worried, Rosamond; it's just that Mr Thompson would then have your name and description all over Guildford by suppertime tonight.'

'In which case, I certainly don't want to meet him. Once I'm established here, hopefully I can attend church with you without comment.' She picked up her bag and followed her friend to the landing and down a passageway.

'This is my chamber when I stay,' said Claire. 'Would you like to take the one adjacent, or would you prefer somewhere more private?'

'I should prefer to be next door to you, and I'm in no position to quibble anyway, being an unwanted guest.'

'Unexpected perhaps, but definitely not unwanted. Your being here will make this stay a pleasure rather than several weeks of tedium. I suppose it's fortunate my aunt still keeps two footmen and is thus able to be transported to and from the drawing room each day.'

The room that was to become Rosamond's home for the next few weeks was more than adequate. It had all the necessary furniture, and there was even a small anteroom in which to wash. 'I'll be very happy here, thank you. If you would kindly show me the linen cupboard I'll make my bed whilst you speak to your aunt. I'll remain here until you send word the visitor has gone.'

Making her own bed was a novel experience and not nearly as simple as she'd imagined. By the time she'd managed to place the first sheet and put the pillowcases on smoothly, she was hot and cross. The expected knock to summon her downstairs came too soon — her hair was in disarray and was decorated with several feathers. She ignored it and continued her battle with the bed linen.

★ ★ ★

Elliott hammered loudly on the front door. His heart was pumping and his hands were clammy. What if she refused to return? He couldn't force her to come back, and whilst she remained under this roof he could hardly take the bed and solve the problem once and for all.

They were taking an unconscionable time to answer the wretched door. He grabbed the knocker precisely as someone pulled the door open, and he almost fell headlong into the arms of an elderly woman. He regained his balance before the unfortunate lady had recovered from the shock.

'Good afternoon. I wish to speak to Miss Winters immediately.' The woman seemed unimpressed by his demand. 'I am Colonel Bromley. It's a matter of extreme importance.' Not allowing her to refuse, he stepped into the entrance hall and marched across it, leaving her no option but to close the door behind him.

'The mistress is not receiving, sir. She's indisposed.' The housekeeper — for she could be none other — glanced nervously at the half-open double doors to his right.

He raised his voice to parade-ground level. 'My visit also concerns a Miss Browning, who I believe is a relative of Miss Winters.'

This got the desired result. 'Show the man in, Jones. Don't leave him to kick his heels in the hallway.' Miss Winters might be indisposed, but her voice had lost none of its clarity.

He didn't wait to be announced but strode across, tapped once on the door, and stepped in. He was confronted by a beady-eyed, incredibly ancient lady stretched out on a day bed. He bowed and heard the door close behind him.

'Well, Colonel Bromley, what do you want with my niece?' She waved towards the chair on her right and he sat.

'I would like to have your promise that not a word of what I tell you will leave this room.'

She nodded. 'You have my full attention, young man.'

'I am the Duke of Hathersage, but I am also Colonel Bromley.' If he had announced he was an escapee from a lunatic asylum she couldn't have been more surprised.

'Now I am intrigued, your grace, as to what a gentleman of your importance is doing in my humble abode.'

Briefly he explained the whole. For some reason he trusted this old lady with their secret and had no wish to lie to her. 'Miss Browning will arrive with my wife at any moment, madam, and I would like somewhere we could converse in private, if you would be so kind.'

Before she could reply the door opened and a young lady stepped in. He was on his feet to greet Rosamond but the girl was alone. She stared at him in puzzlement. 'I beg your pardon, Aunt Agatha. I thought you had the vicar with you.'

He bowed. 'Allow me to introduce myself, Miss Browning. I am Colonel Elliott Edward Bromley, the Duke of Hathersage.' She sank into a graceful curtsy but appeared unable to respond. He stepped forward and raised her up. 'I apologise for causing you distress, but I believe you can help me in my search for my wife.'

'Oh my goodness! I understand it all now. Rosamond is running away from you, your grace. She believes she is no longer worthy to be your wife.'

It was his turn to be rendered momentarily speechless. He hadn't expected this information to be shared so readily — there must be something about this family that inspired confidence. 'As you know the whole, I'll tell you why I'm here. I don't give a d — fig about anything apart from the fact that I love Rosamond and that she is, whether she wishes it or not, remaining my duchess.'

'In which case, your grace, you will find her grace upstairs. I left her attempting to make a bed in the third chamber on the right.'

'Thank you. You were God-sent, Miss Browning, and you will have my undying gratitude for taking in my wife and keeping her from harm.'

'Go to her, your grace, but I warn you she will not easily be persuaded. She's convinced she must make her life elsewhere and is *persona non grata* at Hathersage.'

He turned to Miss Winters. 'Madam, do I have your permission to venture upstairs?'

'Go ahead, your grace. There's not been so much excitement here since my pug dog bit the vicar.'

Today was turning out to be quite extraordinary in every way. He was at a loss to understand why two such rational people as himself and Rosamond had thought it proper to reveal their dirty laundry to complete strangers. His mouth twitched. Neither Rosamond nor he had been behaving in a sensible fashion these past few days, so perhaps discovering his wife in a bedchamber doing the work of the chambermaid was only to be expected.

He counted the doors and stopped outside the third one. His hands were shaking like a blancmange; he wasn't as sure about the outcome as he'd professed. He tapped on the door and, not waiting for her to give him permission to enter, stepped inside. He carefully turned the key, removed it from the lock and slipped it into his waistcoat pocket.

Rosamond was unaware of his entrance, which gave him time to regain his composure. She was looking absolutely adorable: her cheeks were becomingly flushed and her glorious hair was tumbling over her shoulders. She was muttering to herself and flapping and banging at a recalcitrant bed sheet.

'Would you like me to assist you, my darling? I would imagine this is the first time in your life that you've attempted to make a bed.' He remained with his back against the door, made no effort to approach, and waited for her reaction.

'How did you get in here? I've no wish to speak to you — not now, not ever. Our association is at an end. Lady Rosamond Hathersage, the girl that you married, no longer exists either legally or in any other way.'

'You're talking fustian, my love, and well you know it. Whatever the circumstances of your birth, your father acknowledged you. As far as he was concerned you were his daughter.'

She remained unconvinced by his rhetoric. 'I don't care about such niceties, your grace. I have no Hathersage blood in me, and the man I loved and called my father wished for one of his legitimate daughters to marry you.' She raised her hand as he made a move towards her. 'I understand now why he set up my trust fund as he did; why he encouraged me to write and didn't push me to have a season.'

This was not going the way he'd planned. She was speaking nothing but the truth. When the late duke made that will, he'd known Rosamond had vowed she wouldn't marry, and therefore his intention had indeed been for him to marry one of the other girls.

★ ★ ★

She was watching him closely and knew exactly at what point he understood she was right. She wanted to throw herself at him, tell him she didn't care about bloodlines or the will, but she couldn't. However difficult it was for both of them, he must accept what couldn't be changed and leave her to find a new path.

'Elliott, I'll always love you, but that is now irrelevant. You must go away. Explain to my half-sisters why our marriage must be dissolved and try and forget we ever met. You have responsibilities now; you cannot please yourself, however much you might wish to.'

His face crumpled and his look of devastation broke her heart anew. There was nothing she could do or say that would improve the situation. 'Goodbye, your grace. Go with my blessing and my wish that you'll soon forget me and find happiness with Lady Amelia.' Her voice cracked and she couldn't continue.

He was as distressed as she. 'I accept what you're saying is right, but I'm not sure I can do as you say. How can I take your sister as my wife when I'll always love you?'

'You are the Duke of Hathersage. You must do what's necessary to protect your inheritance. I'll remain here as long as I can, and will send my address to you when I move. There might well be legal matters that require me to be present.' They both understood she was referring to a medical examination to prove she was a maiden still.

'I'm not giving up without a fight, Rosamond. There must be something we can do to satisfy the requirements of the will and still remain together.' Angrily he brushed his eyes, and his throat convulsed. 'There's one thing I can and will do, sweetheart: I'll arrange for your trust fund to be released immediately. If that's not possible then I'll settle an annuity on you myself. I'm not having the woman I love living in penury.' His voice was gruff and he was using every ounce of his self-control not to move away from the door and take her in his arms.

'Very well, your grace. I should be most grateful for your financial assistance in this matter. My adopted father must have intended me to have the money, and I'll take it for his sake.'

She turned her back on him and ran into the dressing room. She collapsed against the door and buried her face in her hands and could no longer control her sobs. The door moved a little; he was trying to get in and comfort her.

She pressed her feet against the floor and pushed the door with her back. After a few moments he gave up and the bedroom door slammed shut behind him.

There was nothing he could do to mend matters. If only they had consummated the marriage, they could have remained together — but at what cost? Her sisters' lives would be ruined, they would be tainted by her illegitimacy, and any children she and Elliott might have had would never be accepted in the ton. They must both put their personal happiness to one side and do what was right, however heartbreakingly difficult this was for both of them.

15

Rosamond woke stiff and uncomfortable from sitting on the floor with her back to the door. She pulled herself upright but remained leaning on the wall, trying to marshal her thoughts and decide what she should be doing next. She was cold, ached all over, and her limbs were as heavy as lead.

Like an old woman, she struggled to open the door and moved wearily into her temporary bedchamber. She looked around in surprise; someone had completed the bed-making, closed the shutters and drawn the curtains. There was even a cheerful applewood fire. In the centre of room was a table with a crisp white cloth and a covered supper tray.

Claire and her aunt were being too kind to her. She had no appetite, but hadn't eaten since yesterday, and she had no wish to become unwell and a burden to someone else. She removed the cloth and saw an appetising display of items: a miniature slice of game pie, a handful of strawberries, a freshly baked roll and a small wedge of cheese, plus a plate of tiny, lovingly decorated cakes. A jug of elderflower cordial completed the delicious array. Her stomach rumbled in anticipation and she pulled out the chair, unfolded the napkin and took a tentative nibble of the game pie.

She decided to taste a little of everything; it would be uncivil not to when someone had gone to so much trouble. When she'd finished there was little left. For a short while she'd been able to forget and enjoy her meal. Now she wanted to sleep. Maybe things would seem a little less bleak in the morning.

After a short struggle to remove her gown, she slipped on the waiting nightgown and crawled into bed expecting to lie awake and be forced to relive everything that had happened in the past week. In fact she was asleep minutes after getting into bed and was roused the next morning by someone drawing the curtains and opening the shutters.

'Good morning, Miss Jamieson. There's the bath drawn next door if you would care to come through.'

Rosamond shot up in bed and gaped at the speaker. 'What are you doing here, Jane? I don't understand.'

Her maid smiled sadly. 'His grace has arranged for me to stay with you. There are also two footmen, two parlour maids, a groom and a stable boy, all from Hathersage. When you set up your own establishment you will already have your own loyal staff to run it for you.' The girl dabbed her eyes on her apron. 'It's not right, none of this, but at least his grace is making sure you're well looked after.'

'This is appalling, Jane. I can't just foist half a dozen extra servants onto poor Miss Winters. Whatever was he thinking of?' She scrambled out of bed, her head buzzing with the possible complications. 'Why do I need grooms?'

'His grace has sent a gig and a saddle horse for your use. Miss Winters is delighted to have the extra help and not have to pay for it herself. They'll soon have this place spick and span, miss, and you'll feel more at home with familiar faces around you.'

'I should love a bath, but where on earth have you put it? There's certainly no space in the little adjoining room.'

'Miss Winters and Miss Browning are relocating you, Miss Jamieson. There's a pretty apartment with a dressing room and decent-sized closet that you're to use during your stay here. All your belongings have been transferred from Hathersage and your chambermaid is putting everything away at this very moment.'

For Elliott to show her such kindness was almost too much. It would be far easier if he treated her with the disdain she'd expected; then perhaps she could move forward and try and put him in her past. Having her own staff constantly around her was going to make this impossible. But she could hardly throw back his generous gesture; he was heartbroken too, so she would accept his help graciously for the moment.

Jane led her to the other end of the house and into a delightful sitting room which overlooked the garden. Adjoining this chamber was a bedroom of similar size to the one she'd first occupied. However, there was a large dressing room where her bath awaited her, plus a generous cupboard for her clothes. Rosamond glanced in as she walked past and was surprised to see the shelves and hooks bursting with garments.

The bath did nothing to revive her spirits; she was even more lethargic when she was assisted from it. Her head appeared to be full of wool and she couldn't concentrate — but far worse, she was scarcely able to place one foot in front of the other without help. Was she going down with a summer fever? One thing was sure, she hadn't the energy to get up today.

Strangely, Jane didn't quibble when she told her but folded back the crisp, clean sheets and helped her settle in. 'I don't require any breakfast,' Rosamond said. 'I should like to sleep.'

'I'll only be in the dressing room, miss. If you need anything just call out.'

* * *

Elliott clenched his fist and was about to take a swing at Davenport when he saw sympathy reflected in his friend's eyes. He lowered his arm and slumped back into his chair. 'I apologise. I'm not myself. If you want to cut and run I shouldn't blame you.'

'I shouldn't have sprung it on you like that, but Dawkins was most insistent you knew immediately.'

'Let me get this straight — as long as I don't start the process of annulment, I can continue to run the estate? However, once the proceedings are underway, everything is in abeyance once more.' He slammed his hands on the table and it disintegrated. They both ignored the wreckage. 'What in God's name am I to do? I must marry Lady Amelia in order to have funds, but as soon as I begin the process I shall be penniless again.'

'Another thing you haven't considered, Bromley, is that it might well take over a year to have your marriage dissolved. Also, these proceedings will soon become common knowledge, and everything you're trying to protect will be undone.' He remained two paces away just in case he decided to take another swing at him.

'I can see no way out of this conundrum. Rosamond is determined that her adoptive father should have his way. She would rather see us reduced to misery for the remainder of our lives, than go against his wishes.'

They were interrupted by a hesitant

knock on the door and he roared at whoever was there to go away. There was a second polite knock on the door and Davenport walked over and opened it. The lawyer peered round the door nervously.

'I beg your pardon, your grace, but I must speak to you most urgently.'

'Then come in if you must. Make it brief — I've no wish to listen to hours of boring legalities today.' He was being boorish and intimidating but he couldn't help himself. One moment he was in dark despair, the next in a fury, and this was closely followed by an insane desire to run away and leave this tangle behind for someone else to sort out.

'Might I be permitted to sit down, your grace?'

Elliott looked more closely at the lawyer and saw his face was grey, his eyes bloodshot, and he was scarcely able to stay upright without clutching the edge of the desk. He shook his head and rubbed his eyes.

'Please, Mr Dawkins, be seated. I apologise for my appalling rudeness — you look dead on your feet.' He glanced enquiringly at his friend, who understood his unspoken request immediately.

'I'll send for refreshments. We've all been awake too long, and without either eating or drinking anything substantial.'

The lawyer sat with a grateful sigh. 'Your grace, I've discovered Lady Rosamond's birth certificate. It doesn't matter what the dowager duchess claims to be the truth; the evidence states otherwise. The late duke recognised her as his daughter and she was registered as such. I'm certain there are many children of the aristocracy whose parentage does not warrant too close a scrutiny. However, once a child is recognised it makes no odds in the eyes of the law how they were conceived. Lady Rosamond is a legitimate daughter, with as much right to the title as any of her sisters.'

He held out a parchment.

'I can't believe it. I'm sure that witch has no notion he legitimised Rosamond. So my marriage to her can stand — I've fulfilled the requirements of the will by marrying her.' He blinked away his tears. His life wasn't ruined; he could be with the woman he loved, and all because the old duke had accepted his wife's by-blow as his own.

The rattle of crockery heralded the arrival of much-needed sustenance. 'I'll never be able to thank you, Mr Dawkins. It might have been weeks before I discovered that document amongst the trunk-loads we have yet to search through.' Two footmen staggered in with laden trays and, finding the table in pieces on the carpet, looked round for somewhere else to put them. 'On the sideboard. Send word to the stables that I'll require my horse in half an hour.' He rubbed his hand over his bristly chin and reconsidered. 'No, in two hours.'

Davenport returned and Elliott quickly

explained the situation. His friend looked almost as delighted as he was. 'So the marriage will stand? Lady Rosamond can return and everything is well?'

'Indeed it is, and you don't have to tell me how relieved you are. I'm not blind to the fact that you and Amelia have formed an attachment. If Mr Dawkins hadn't found the birth certificate, four people would have had their lives ruined.'

There was no more conversation for a while as they tucked into the delicious spread sent up from the kitchens. After three plates and a jug of coffee, Elliott was feeling almost human again. 'You and Millie are in the clear, my friend, whatever happens between Rosamond and me. However, I've yet to convince her that remaining married to me won't be going against the wishes of my predecessor.' He tossed his napkin onto his empty plate and heaved himself upright. He'd not slept for thirty-six hours but after a bath, a shave and a change of raiment, he would be ready to ride to Guildford.

'Lady Rosamond — I beg your pardon, your duchess — has her people about her,' said Davenport. 'She is in a comfortable house and will come to no harm if you leave your visit until after you've slept. Why turn up exhausted? Far better to leave it until tomorrow.'

'I'm not such a weakling I can't manage without sleep for a day or two. Good God, man, we've done it dozens of times before and come to no harm.'

'On campaign one must do whatever it takes to win the battle. Your war is won; you now have to negotiate a peace, and that would be better done with a clear head and a good night's sleep.'

He was about to refuse when he saw the sense in his friend's suggestion. Perhaps being apart from him for another day might weaken her resolve and make his task easier. He came to a sudden decision. 'You speak sense, Davenport. I'll take the carriage tomorrow to collect her. Now, I think we must all get some sleep.' He smiled at the exhausted lawyer. 'I trust you will be feeling sufficiently refreshed to join us for dinner tonight?' The man was struggling to regain his feet and Elliott took his arm and helped him out of his chair.

'I should be delighted to join you, your grace, and will certainly be quite well by this evening.'

'Will you inform the young ladies for me, Davenport? I'll send word to the stables and then retire to my apartment until dinnertime.'

* * *

The room was strangely peaceful, the distant sounds of carriages and diligences unfamiliar, but somehow reassuring. Rosamond mulled over the most recent of the unexpected events that had rocked her previously uneventful life.

Her mother's antipathy was now understandable — had she thought her husband had kept her unwanted and illegitimate daughter in the family in order to remind her of her indiscretion? What was also clear was the reason the duke had never left Hathersage, even for a night: he had no longer trusted his wife to remain faithful.

They had gone on to have two further children, Flora and Elizabeth, and Rosamond had never doubted for a moment they were deeply attached to each other. It seemed impossible a man could forgive his wife for betraying him and continue to live with her as if nothing had happened. Yet her adoptive father had not only done so, but also brought her up as his own. Indeed, he'd actually singled her out for extra attention.

Had this been because he wished to make things difficult for her mother? No, it had been because he'd seen Rosamond was treated unkindly by her only parent. She wiped her eyes on the sheet. It didn't seem credible that any man could love a woman so much that he could forgive her such a dreadful sin. Rosamond's disgrace was not of her own making. Did this mean she could also be accepted back into the fold? Could this mean there was a glimmer of hope for her and Elliott?

She threw back the covers and called for Jane. 'I wish to get up after all. I must go downstairs immediately and speak to Miss Winters and Miss Browning. I don't know what I was thinking of, languishing in bed as if I was an invalid when Miss Winters is carried down each day with a broken leg.'

Once dressed, she hurried through the house in search of her new friend. The drawing room doors were open and she knocked.

'Come in, my dear. I'm so glad you decided to join us. Far better to get on with your life and not pine for what you cannot have.' Miss Winters was comfortably established on the chaise-longue, but of her friend there was no sign.

'That's sound advice, madam, and I intend to do my best to follow it. Might I join you for a while? Is there something you would like me to do for you?'

'There's nothing for you to do. You are my honoured house guest and have brought much-needed excitement to my dull existence.' She pointed to the chair placed opposite her position. 'My niece has gone with one of your maids to increase my usual order with our supplier. With so many extra mouths to feed, we would soon be on short commons indeed if I don't do something about it today.'

This was exactly what Rosamond feared. 'I know his grace just wishes me to be comfortable, but he hasn't considered the financial implications. I have five guineas; I insist that I — '

'Absolutely no need to consider such a thing, Miss Jamieson. A very substantial sum is to be paid into my account every month that you remain here. Indeed, my dear girl, I'm not famous for my profligacy, but I rather think I'm going to enjoy spending someone else's money on luxuries.'

This outrageous statement made Rosamond smile. 'In which case, I'll say no more about it. However, there is one thing I would like to make clear. I have no intention of attending morning calls, card parties or the like. I wish to remain quietly here and, if you have visitors, I shan't be present.'

The old lady nodded vigorously. 'Of course you have no wish to socialise at the moment — but perhaps in a few months you might feel differently.'

'Yes, quite possibly I will. Thank you for being so understanding. If you would excuse me for a while, I should like to familiarise myself with my new home.'

'Run along, my dear. You must do as you please. I'm sure you wish to see your people, and they certainly are eager to ascertain for themselves that you are well.'

The footmen waiting for her in the

vestibule bowed, but being from Hathersage, knew how to behave and made no attempt to converse with her. She smiled and nodded and wandered through the house, peering into rooms and examining closets. Eventually she arrived at the side door and found it unlocked. She would visit the stables and see which horse had been sent for her use.

The sound of voices and the clatter of hooves made finding her way much easier. Her eyes prickled — she wished she could have Sultan and Calli here with her. They would be safe enough for the moment, but when her finances were sorted and she could set up her own establishment, she would definitely send for them.

A moss-covered path led around the side of the building to a small archway. She stepped through and looked around with interest. The coach house was open-fronted and contained the smartly painted gig that had been for the sole use of the dowager duchess.

This required a pair of carriage horses and a driver, and had room for four passengers. Any carriage was obliged to pass through the yard and into the turning circle before being able to exit.

At the far end of this building were several store-rooms, no doubt for fodder, tack and the other essential items necessary for keeping horses. Although the paint was peeling, the cobbles were freshly swept and there were a row of equine heads hanging over the loose box doors.

A stable boy she didn't recognise touched his cap and scampered off. She was surprised the groom didn't make an appearance, but then she understood. They would have been told she was no longer to be addressed as either 'my lady' or 'your grace' but would be reluctant to call her Miss Jamieson.

They would have to become used to it; they couldn't hide from her indefinitely. Peggy, the pretty grey mare usually ridden by Millie, stood in the first box. She was unsurprised to see that the second two contained the pair of matched bay geldings which had been a gift to the dowager from her husband. In the last box was another handsome bay gelding; this one must be for the groom's use when he accompanied her on her rides.

She walked from one to the other, patting and stroking and enjoying the non-judgemental company of her favourite animals. Then there was the sound of horses approaching and, before she could escape, a familiar team of chestnuts began to turn in through the archway.

16

There would be a moment before the driver of the vehicle could see her. She ran across the yard and back through the archway. Where should she hide? The vegetable garden — nobody would think to look for her there, as the paths were overgrown and not at all suitable for a young lady dressed in a delicate muslin gown. She pushed her way through the weeds and nettles, snagging her skirt several times and being stung more often than that by the vicious green leaves. Her heart was beating painfully in her chest, her hands damp, and she still wasn't safe from discovery.

There was a dilapidated building at the far end of the plot that would be ideal. She threaded her way there, no longer caring if she ruined her dress, just desperate to be somewhere Elliott couldn't find her. She wasn't strong enough to refuse to return to him if she saw him again. A sharp pain tore into her calf but she ignored it. There was the remnant of a door and she scrambled past it into the gloomy interior. This was packed full of tools and garden implements from the days when Miss Winters had employed sufficient outside staff to grow vegetables, as well as tend to the lawn and shrubbery.

She hid herself in the far corner and sat down on a pile of old sacks. She prayed they would think she'd gone into town to meet Claire and not begin a search. Why had he come again today? Didn't he realise he was making matters so much worse by prolonging the agony of their separation? Her leg throbbed and she pulled aside the torn skirt of her gown to examine the injury. Her head spun at the sight of so much blood. Something had sliced deep into her calf and she needed urgent medical attention.

She mustn't panic; what would she

have done if this had been one of her sisters in this predicament? She must apply firm pressure to the wound and elevate the limb. She ripped off the lower half of her petticoat and then tore it into strips. With shaking hands she folded one into a pad and pressed it against the gaping cut, then quickly bound the remaining strips tightly around her leg.

Her eyes had become accustomed to the darkness of the interior and she could see there were several upturned flowerpots, which would be ideal to prop under her leg. She just had to shuffle forward a little and would be in a suitable position. Her hands were scratched from the brambles and painful from the nettles, but these were of no consequence compared to her other injury.

Once she was resettled, with her back supported by a criss-cross of garden tools, she thought the crisis had been averted for the moment. However, she wasn't foolish enough to imagine her makeshift bandage would be adequate for more than a short while. Would anyone hear her if she shouted for help? She strained her ears but couldn't hear anything, apart from birdsong and the gentle rustling of leaves. She was too far from the house and stables to have any hope of attracting attention — she must pray Elliott would decide to wait until Claire returned and not drive away.

★　★　★

Elliott remained on the steps outside the house until he was sure Albert could negotiate the narrow archway successfully. As he didn't intend to stay for any longer than it took to collect his wife, he'd been tempted to leave the carriage waiting outside. However, the steep lane was too narrow to allow another vehicle to pass, so he had no option but to tell his coachman to take the vehicle through the arch.

Someone must have observed his arrival, as the front door opened before he reached the top step. A familiar footman bowed. 'Your grace, Miss Winters is receiving in the drawing room.'

'Where is my duchess? I've come to take her home. No doubt everyone from Hathersage will wish to accompany her — you can return in the gig.'

The lad looked bemused, and well he might, for yesterday Rosamond had been Miss Jamieson and now she was mysteriously the duchess again. 'Her grace, I believe, went to view the horses.'

'Show his grace in here at once.' The garrulous old lady couldn't be ignored.

He marched into the drawing room without bothering to knock. 'Miss Winters, you'll be delighted to know that . . . that . . . the misunderstanding that led to my wife being here is now resolved. I've come to collect her immediately. I hope that you will accept three months' remuneration as compensation for your inconvenience.'

Her frown changed instantly to a

happy smile. 'I shall be delighted to accept your generous offer, your grace. The duchess went to the stables. I'm sure you will find her there.'

He nodded politely and strode off to find his beloved wife. The stable boy said Rosamond had been talking to the horses, but he had no idea where she was at present. Elliott grinned — she would have made a bolt for it when she saw the chestnuts. He didn't blame her. If he hadn't been able to take her back as his wife, seeing her would have almost killed him.

He walked into the garden and called her name, but got no response. He swore under his breath. Of course she wouldn't answer; there would be little point in her hiding if she revealed herself when he called. He could hardly shout across the garden that everything had been resolved, and that she wasn't illegitimate after all. He chuckled and began a systematic search. He could move silently when he had to, and if he wanted to find her he must approach without her knowledge.

After half an hour he had scoured the garden but not found her. She must have gone out; he would return to the house and make further enquiries. He met Miss Browning in the vestibule. 'Is Rosamond with you? Everything has been resolved; I've come to take her home. I've searched the damned garden from end to end and wonder if she has slipped in unnoticed and could be hiding somewhere indoors.'

The girl curtsied. 'You are welcome to search the house, your grace. I'll immediately get the staff involved. I'm sure we'll find her very soon.'

A further twenty minutes later and she was still not found. 'Miss Browning, is there anywhere in the garden I might have missed?' They were standing at the open French doors, looking out, as he spoke.

'Did you search the vegetable patch over there? It's just possible she went in there, but it's so overgrown — '

He didn't wait to hear the end of her

sentence but jumped the five steps from the terrace and raced across the grass, down an overgrown path, and hurdled the raggedy hedge. He could see nothing through the brambles and overgrown weeds — it could take hours to find her. 'Rosamond, darling, don't hide from me. Everything is resolved. Rosamond, are you in here?'

A faint voice replied from somewhere on the far side of the garden. 'Elliott, I'm in the building in the corner. I prayed you'd come and find me. I cannot come to you, for I'm seriously injured.'

He barged across the garden, tearing out the weeds with his bare hands to make himself a pathway. He saw the building immediately and was at the entrance in seconds. He tore the broken door from its hinges. He clutched the door frame and his stomach churned. Rosamond was collapsed against some old hoes and rakes with her left leg raised on a garden pot. The makeshift bandage she'd applied was blood-soaked.

'I've got you now, my love. I'll take care of your injury. Hold on to my neck and I'll carry you to the house.'

'I love you, Elliott, and have decided to offer you *carte blanche*. Not fair to Millie, but I don't want to live without you.' Her words were barely audible and she spoke no more. Her head flopped horribly on his shoulder as he ran towards the house. Was he too late? Surely God couldn't be so cruel as to snatch her away after all they'd been through these past two days?

He shouted to Miss Browning, who had seen him approaching. 'I need a needle and thread, a boiling kettle, clean cloths and a jug-ful of watered wine.' The girl raised her hand in acknowledgement and ran inside. He could hear her issuing instructions as he approached.

He didn't stop in the garden room but headed upstairs, where Jane guided him into a bedchamber where the bed was already turned back and clean towels placed across it. He gently placed his unconscious burden down and quickly pushed the pile of pillows beneath her injured limb. 'I need to suture the injury to her leg. I've done this many times before on campaign; there are never enough medics to deal with the minor injuries.'

'What do you require, your grace?'

'Can you remove her gown and the worst of the grime from her leg? I must go downstairs to collect what I need but will be back momentarily.'

The fine silver needle and silk thread were boiled in the kettle whilst he scrubbed his hands and washed his arms. An army surgeon had explained to him that using clean instruments and having clean hands for some inexplicable reason appeared to prevent infection. This wasn't always possible in the heat of battle, but today he would follow this strange advice.

He filled the bowl with boiling water and then extracted the needle and thread, being careful not to touch them overmuch. With the things he needed on a tray, he returned to Rosamond. Miss Browning and the maid had done as he'd requested and his patient was now awake and sipping the drink he'd instructed to be brought to her. He hoped she'd remained comatose until after he'd sewn her up.

'You must close your eyes and hold tight to Miss Browning's hand. This is going to hurt, my darling, but if I don't close your wound, it could prove disastrous.'

'I've already had two glasses of delicious wine so I don't care what you do.' She smiled and his heart flipped.

'Miss Browning, has that wine been watered?'

'No, your grace. I thought it better if her grace was a bit tipsy during the procedure.'

Small wonder Rosamond had taken to this girl so quickly — she was a sensible and intelligent young woman. 'When I uncover the injury I need you to press these pads of material firmly on either side. Do you understand?' She nodded. He pushed all other considerations to one side and, gritting his teeth, cut through the bandage.

The girl was ready and, although blood flowed freely for a moment, her pressure stemmed this. Rosamond was humming to herself and seemed oblivious. He steadied his breathing and put in the first stitch. She barely flinched and so he hemmed her cut as neatly as a seamstress. He held his hand out for a clean wet cloth and carefully cleaned the area. Then he placed a dry dressing on the wound and carefully bound it up again.

'There, I think the danger's over. You've lost a deal of blood, sweetheart, but I'm certain in a day or two you'll be as good as new.'

Miss Browning and the maid carefully removed the blood-stained towels from beneath her, propped the leg on pillows once again, and then pulled up the bed covers. 'I've taken the precaution of sending for the doctor, your grace, but I doubt he'll be needed.'

'I hope not, and I thank you, Miss Browning, for your assistance. Could I ask you to send a message to the stables that I won't be leaving today? The coachman will have to return the day after tomorrow. I'm certain she'll be well enough to travel by then.'

The girl curtsied and left him alone with his wife. He hooked off his boots, shrugged out of his jacket, removed his stock and prepared to join her on the bed. 'Well, darling, shall we get drunk together?'

She giggled and offered him her empty glass. 'I've had two already. You will have to catch up.' She stared blearily at him. 'Exactly why are you here, Elliott? I don't understand what's going on.'

'I shall drink my quota and then we can share until the jug's empty.' She was so incredibly beautiful, even pale and scratched. She was breathtaking. He downed the wine, refilled the glass and then climbed onto the bed. 'You are legitimate. Your father registered you as his daughter, so whatever your pernicious mother might have said, we can ignore it. Our marriage stands and you remain my wife.'

'I'm Lady Rosamond again?' She frowned delightfully as if presented with an insoluble puzzle.

'No, sweetheart, you are the Duchess of Hathersage. Lady Rosamond is no more.'

'I love you, darling Elliott. I don't care if my leg falls off, as long as I can be with you.'

'I seem to recall that you offered to be my mistress?'

'I did, didn't I? However, I shall prefer being your wife.' She reached out and tugged at his shirt. 'Exactly when will this be, do you think?'

'Don't look at me like that, darling girl. There's nothing on this earth I'd rather do than make love to you right now, but you've got nine stitches in your leg — '

She pulled his head down and kissed

him. His control was melting like snow in the sun. This was madness — Miss Browning was bringing the doctor in at any moment. He must resist.

'Fiddlesticks to that, my love. I don't believe that becoming your true wife in any way involves my injured leg.' Her fingers slid into his hair and caressed his skull. She dropped little kisses along his jaw and his resistance collapsed.

'I love you to distraction. You are my life, and together we shall manage Hathersage and name our first son in honour of your father.'